What p
Twenty-

I enjoyed Peter Honey's delightful short stories. So inventive, varied and entertaining. LADY BALL

I am not fond of books of short stories but I have enjoyed Peter Honey's atmospheric scene-setting and his humorous denouements! LYNN BINDMAN

Anyone who enjoys Maupassant and Somerset Maugham will fall on this scintillating collection with a whoop. Peter Honey's stories are unfailingly entertaining, stimulating, funny and often surprising. PROFESSOR TIM BLANNING

The stories are excellent; ingenious, imaginative and not over-written. I think I smiled, or even laughed, on every last page. ALAN CHANCE

I enjoyed the stories with the quirky Peter Honey, humour I recognise. JO CUMMING

I thoroughly enjoyed the twists and turns of the plots, the sometimes comic turns of phrase (which had me belly-laughing) and the fine use of the English language. The book was a pleasure to read. COLIN DOAK

I'm glad to report that the book has passed the bath test. I read the short stories with rapt attention and the book remained dry as a bone. RICHARD FARRANT

Peter Honey's stories embrace the lives of many of us, triggering memories, or at least thoughts, of the might have been. Digestibly short and fun. NICHOLAS HALTON

Peter Honey's short stories are a welcome relief from my excessive diet of stodgy non-fiction. KEN JONES

These stories are delightful 15 minute reads. Peter Honey writes fluently with gentle humour about ordinary events happening in ordinary people's lives, and each story leaves the reader with a mischievous smile at the end. PROFESSOR ANDREW MAYO

This little book is fabulous. Every story so different. A lesson to learn from some. Others very amusing. I can't wait for the next book! ADRIENNE SACKIN

Original stories that keep you guessing until the last page, illuminated by an elegant writing style, with small things well observed. PETER SIDDALL

I love the stories! A wonderful range, fun, mischievous, if not racy at times. You won't be able to read just one at a time, since you'll have to know the next wonderful piece of ingenuity. ROBERT WILSON

Twenty-five More Short Stories

Ray
Enjoy!
Peter

Peter Honey

Dec 2023

First Edition published 2023
by
2QT Limited (Publishing)
Stockport, United Kingdom
Copyright © Peter Honey 2023

Cover design by Charlotte Mouncey with illustration by Peter Honey

Printed in Great Britain by TJ Books Limited

A CIP catalogue record for this book is available from the British Library

ISBN - 978-1-7395555-6-6

For Carol Ann and in memory of our daughter,
Susan, 1966-1980

Contents

Foreword

Every writer approaches things differently. P. G. Wodehouse used to lay out a complete diagram showing every character and each of their interactions, and then, with the plot and all its complex twists laid out, he would set about the writing. Peter says he has no idea where a story will go when he begins; he just starts and then sees how things develop. Here are a few of the opening lines of the stories in this collection. If you think you can guess where they lead, you may also be able to bend spoons with your thoughts.

'Dennis gave a whoop of joy when his wife, Alice, told him she was pregnant.'

'Once upon a time an entrepreneur called Dr Do had a brilliant idea.'

'A litter picking stick was one of the many things Daphne's husband left behind when he suddenly died.'

I've been an avid reader all my life - novels, short stories, plays, history, scientific, etc. - upwards of a hundred books a year, and volumes of short stories make up five or ten percent of that reading. Needless to say, some short story collections are so-so, some are good, and some sparkle. This little volume of 25 short stories falls into the last category. They remind me of the short stories of O. Henry which have a characteristic twist in the tail (or is it "tale"?). Every story in this collection is different. Every story is engaging. Some will get you laughing out loud, some will tug at your heart, some will stagger you with their creativity and set you to wondering about the sort of mind that could think of something so clever.

It's not uncommon for so-called short stories not to be short at all. Many might almost be called novellas. Not so with this collection. They don't go beyond a few pages and your interest won't flag; you know there is going to be some sort of unexpected ending and the story becomes more and more compelling as you try to think what it might turn out to be. I never guessed any of the endings. I doubt you will either.

One piece of advice: try not to read more than one story a day. Roll each one around in your mind and savour its delights before you consume the next one. That will give you twenty-five wonderful experiences. With his first volume of short stories I rationed myself to one a day, which I read at the end of the day after all work was finished, and while enjoying my evening drink (note the singular). The temptation to repeat the sequence - finish work, pour drink, read story - was high, but I was happily able to reach a compromise and put down the book while picking up another drink (do I hear the health police knocking?).

It's customary to see a short piece "About the author" on the back cover of a book. However, this is far from a run-of -the mill book, and Peter Honey is far from a run-of -the mill author. So the publisher will have to decide what else to put on the back cover of this one because here's an attempt to give you at least some idea of what Peter is like.

The thing that's so wonderful about Peter Honey is that he's never outgrown his mischievous wit, and mischievous is the executive word. He is great fun. Who else would list things like, "waist: 34 inches (give or take - mostly give), side of bed: right, failed exam: eleven plus" in his biography? He's wonderful company.

Peter is a polymath of sorts. He's an accomplished and distinguished occupational psychologist, and he's written forty or more academic and professional books, plus innumerable articles, manuals, and booklets. He's the co-developer, with Alan Mumford, of the widely used *Learning Styles Questionnaire*. He's a highly talented water colourist (I'm a proud owner of two of his much admired works). He's a sought after speaker and raconteur. He is also expert at the unexpected: in one instance, a builder of wooden huts and sheds from discarded wood. Equally distant from his other abilities, he's an enthusiastic croquet player (the game Bertie Wooster describes as being "uncannily reminiscent of chess crossed with conkers"). And, beginning with his first volume, (imaginatively titled *Twenty-Five Short Stories*), published in 2021, he is now established as an excellent writer of fiction.

I think it's fair to say that much of this would not be possible without his wonderful, wife, Carol, who keeps things on a (relatively) even keel (exercising what must be the patience of Job and the wisdom of Solomon) while he scurries back and forth keeping all the plates on the long sticks spinning.

Professor Robin Stuart-Kotze, November 2023

Introduction

Since the publication of my first collection of short stories in 2021, I've become hooked. I never meant to carry on. I was going to rest on my laurels, but the habit of producing a story a month, started during lockdown, has become, well, a habit.

Anyway, I couldn't let down my u3a writing group which has continued to meet monthly. They are a demanding lot, not only spotting typos and grammatical errors, but also having the impertinence to urge me to try harder and sometimes to rewrite a story, not just tinker with it. They pay special attention to the endings and are intolerant of stories that simply fizzle out. Any fizzling-out in these stories (I fear some come close) is therefore entirely down to me.

Being hooked on writing short stories is weird. It means you look at everything that happens through the lens of story-telling. Someone tells you an anecdote and you immediately wonder if you could convert it into a story. You trip over an uneven paving stone in the street, or go brambling, or have a casual chat with the man in the laundry, or with the owner of the fruit stall, and you're thinking, 'could this be a story?'

The problem goes deep. You see, I've always been a writer. When I left school, I wrote a novelette (thankfully unpublished) about my schooldays. I've written numerous management books. I've been an agony aunt for *Slimming Magazine*. I've churned out hundreds of monthly articles for training magazines. I've even written my life-story (sorry to deprive you, it's just for family).

Anyway, apart from driving my wife, Carol, mad, why would I stop? Writing is fun and short story writing isn't too onerous. Sometimes people say, 'why don't you write a novel?' but I'd find that a real slog. It's in a different league, and anyway there are already too many novels in the world (probably too many short stories too, but somehow that doesn't seem so profligate).

No, I'll stick to my short stories. They aren't so daunting and I enjoy starting each one afresh, inventing different characters, doing different things. It amuses me - especially as I never know where they'll take me.

Many thanks to Robin Stuart-Kotze for his absurdly generous foreword. In a rare moment of weakness, he offered to give all the stories a final proofread. I've discovered his fondness for commas and his dislike of exclamation marks! (I couldn't resist that one). It's delightfully irresponsible of me to say, if you find any typos, blame Robin.

Recently, in addition to writing short stories, I've taken up writing liquid prose (my version of blank verse). Here's one about short story writing.

How to write short stories

Don't wait to feel inspired and refuse
to be daunted by the blank page.

Write a first sentence with careless abandon
(it doesn't matter what, you'll change it later).

Write another sentence, then another. Keep going.
Get up and stretch every thirty minutes or so.

Be patient when your story gets stuck in a cul-de-sac.
Leave it parked there for a few days while you busy
yourself with other things (perhaps start another story?).

Smile when suddenly you see a (not the) way ahead.
Press on with a flurry of sentences, all the while wondering
where they'll take you and when and how to stop.

Sleep on your story before fiddling and tweaking.
Continue until you're, say, three-quarters satisfied.

Then, don't read the damn thing again for at least a week,
and, when you do, err on the side of leaving well alone.

Be wary of readers who say they like your story.
Doubt their judgement.

That's all there is to it. Happy reading!

Peter Honey, November 2023

The Beta Woman

They're due in half an hour and I'm nervous as hell. They're sending Robert Crampton and a photographer. I've looked up Robert Crampton and it seems he's a well-known *Times* journalist, very well-known in fact. I can see why they're sending him. He has a regular column called *Beta male*. What could be more appropriate, a beta man to interview a beta woman? I've never been interviewed before, except for the occasional job interview and my regular one at the job centre so they can check that I'm still an unemployable wreck, but never by a newspaper or anything like that.

My name is Angela and I'm a GAD. I thought I'd admit that straightaway, like saying, 'My name is Angela and I'm an alcoholic.' Come to think of it, I'd rather be an alcoholic than a GAD. I imagine it would be easier to give up drinking, especially as non-alcoholic drinks are readily available now. My supermarket has a whole area set aside for them.

Yes, I've been diagnosed as having Generalised Anxiety Disorder. Since the pandemic it seems that having GAD has become quite popular. A recent survey by the Mental Health

Foundation found that 73 per cent of us felt anxious 'sometimes' and one in five 'most or all of the time'. It seems that some brains are more sensitive than others - a trait known as 'sensory processing sensitivity'- and, apparently, I've got one of those. It means I'm more sensitive to my surroundings than the normal person (please don't ask me to define 'normal') and this makes me more susceptible to anxiety.

I've known I had a problem for years, ever since I was at primary school, perhaps before that. I was one of those kids who couldn't step on cracks in the pavement and I used to have to wear the same beaded necklace every day or terrible things would happen. I was an only child and looking back I think my mother was over-protective. But I'm not blaming her. She had a tough time, particularly after my dad left to live with another woman. I was only five at the time and of course I thought it was all my fault.

I lacked confidence throughout my teenage years: hopelessly shy, no boyfriends, terrified of exams, convinced I was ugly, lurking in corners keeping out of the limelight, often succumbing to panic attacks when I'd be convinced I was going to die.

I'm 29 now, overweight, economically inactive and anxious about more or less everything. I don't sleep well, convinced that someone has broken into my terraced house and is coming up the stairs. I've got a few friends I've met at various therapy groups I've attended so we've all got similar problems, real or imagined. Silly of me to say that, because if they are imagined they are real, if you see what I mean. If you're not an anxious person I know you'll be thinking 'pull yourself together, woman' or even worse, 'calm down, dear'. Yesterday I saw Piers

Morgan on the telly and he said we should all buck ourselves up and get on the front foot. If only.

As you can imagine, I've read loads of books about anxiety and tried lots of the recommendations: breathing exercises, meditating, yoga, running, reducing my exposure to artificial light, giving up caffeine, white bread and all types of processed food, stopping writing obsessive to-do lists, quitting all social media, not watching the news on the telly, giving up my ritualistic habits such as handwashing, arranging the jars in the kitchen so that they exactly line up, putting towels on the rail in the bathroom so that the labels don't show. Oh, and to stop worrying about being too fat, not having enough money, climate change, rising sea levels, wildfires and so on.

The story of my life: lots of tries, stops and give-ups.

Some of the things I've tried have helped a bit and some not at all, but none have really done the trick. 'The trick', perhaps that's my problem: I'm seeking a magic solution, a cure-all, when probably there isn't one. Only yesterday my therapist (I think she's running out of ideas, scraping the barrel) suggested I should try writing a page or two about how I'm feeling first thing in the morning. Basically, the idea is to dump your anxious thoughts about the day ahead. She gave me some instructions:

Have paper and a biro to hand and, as soon as you wake up, put down every thought that occurs to you, without pausing or thinking too hard. This is 'stream of consciousness' writing. Always write in longhand, never on your laptop. Don't censor or correct anything. The benefit of doing this is that it releases your negativity onto the page so that those thoughts no longer cloud your day. Good luck!

I haven't started doing it yet. I'm too anxious about whether I can relax sufficiently to do anything worthy of being described as 'stream of consciousness'. I know I'll struggle. I'm dyslexic you see and spelling has always been a weakness. I've got used to my laptop correcting everything for me. The idea of having to write in longhand is, well, anxiety-provoking.

Anyway, now that I've been diagnosed it's comforting to have a label; to know I'm not a fraud. Good too, to know I'm not alone. Apparently, there are lots of us. An estimated 1.4 billion people globally have these ultra-sensitive brains.

Only a quarter of an hour now before Robert Crampton is due to arrive with a photographer in tow. A terrifying prospect. I've looked up Robert Crampton on Wikipedia. He's interviewed celebrities like Tony Blair and Paul McCartney. A bit of a come-down being sent to interview me. The people at *The Times* who contacted me to make the arrangements, (I took some persuading - only agreeing when they offered a fee) were keen that I should be interviewed here, at home. A nuisance really because it means I've had to tidy up!

I've got palpitations and I'm not at all sure I can go through with this. I've seen a photograph of Robert Crampton and he definitely looks a bit scary. Perhaps I should draw the curtains and pretend I'm not at home. It's the usual story, I'm in flight-fight mode. My over-sensitive brain is busy misjudging the situation, thinking I'm in danger. I'm telling it (I often talk to my brain) that it's not really an interview, just a friendly chat, but, as usual, it isn't convinced. Maybe they'll want to photograph me in my back garden with all my gear. I've put my trousers on just in case. Why the hell did I agree to do this?

I read a book once about how to access my brain's comfort

zone and release 'feel-good' hormones, such as oxytocin and endorphins. I was assured that if I could do this it would automatically dial-down my levels of anxiety and increase my sense of safety and well-being. The key was neuroplasticity, where I'd rewire my neural pathways and change the chemicals in my brain. It sounds complicated but it all boiled down to accepting, *really* accepting, that I can choose how I react to situations. Choice, that's the key.

I can see why they're sending Robert Crampton. Despite looking rather fierce, it's possible that he's a kindred spirit. Apparently, some years ago he decided to confront his fear of public speaking. Well, I'm assuming it was fear, perhaps it was just incompetence. Anyway he wanted opportunities to practice so he used his newspaper column to advertise himself as a free speaker and got something like 400 replies. He finished up speaking in schools, hospitals, prisons, at a Rotary meeting. He was even invited to preach a sermon and deliver the eulogy at someone's funeral.

I suppose I've done something similar. It's called exposure therapy where you deliberately confront something that makes you anxious and force yourself to do it. The idea is that having done it, your brain realises that it wasn't half as bad as it expected it would be and, hopefully, opts to rewire itself. Hey presto, anxiety conquered. The recommendation is that you pace yourself by doing 'systematic desensitization', a sort of softly, softly, catchee monkey approach.

Since just about everything makes me anxious, I was spoilt for choice when it came to which one to confront. I considered doing some of the suggestions but they all seemed a bit daft, like going into a shop, ordering something and, once it had been wrapped up, saying you'd changed your mind. Or walking down the street blowing bubbles or asking a stranger to lend you some money. Busking was a possibility too, especially as I can't sing. I was still mulling over possibilities when a friend I met at one of the therapy groups - as I told you, all my friends are damaged goods, wrecks the lot of us - sent me an email saying she was raising money for the Samaritans by abseiling down the tower of her parish church. It's a wool church in Norfolk so has a particularly generous tower. I made a small donation but it put the idea of doing something really terrifying, like abseiling, into my head.

I plucked up an abnormal amount of courage and enrolled at an adventure club near me, here in West Sussex. They have a purpose-built abseil tower. Thankfully I had an empathetic instructor who was patient and kind. I told him I was a GAD (he misunderstood me at first and thought I'd said I was glad). Anyway, it wasn't too bad and since then, like my friend, I've done a few charity abseils, mostly down church towers.

Oh God, I think they're here! A car has pulled up outside. Still time to do a runner. No, they've seen me peeping though the curtains. Robert Crampton has given me a wave and the cameraman is unloading a thing that looks like a large, silver umbrella. He's got a searchlight on a stand too. Why did I agree to this?

The coast guards were waiting for me when I got to the bottom. One of them videoed my descent and put it on Facebook. Everyone thinks I'm an absolute nutter abseiling down Beachy Head at dusk, all by myself.

They're ringing the doorbell. They're bound to ask me what's next? Shall I say The Shard?

The Awayday

They'd held their annual company awayday at the same hotel for many years, apart from last year when the hotel had been closed for a major refurbishment.

'I've checked out the hotel. You'll find quite a few changes,' the managing director's PA warned. 'It takes a bit of getting used to.'

'What sort of changes?' Sir Cedric asked, not looking up as he busied himself signing a sheaf of letters with his favourite fountain pen. It had a nib he particularly liked because it converted his signature into a calligraphic masterpiece.

'You'll see,' his PA giggled, carefully blotting each signature before gathering up the letters.

'Ah well, I'm sure we'll cope,' smiled Sir Cedric, putting the lid back on his pen. 'Adapting to change is good for us. Keeps us on our toes.'

Sir Cedric was an orderly man, both in appearance and habits. He cut a distinguished figure with a fine head of white hair parted on the left and a neatly trimmed moustache. He wore bespoke, pinstriped three-piece suits, white shirts and highly polished black shoes. His shirt cuffs protruded sufficiently to expose the gold cufflinks his father had given him on his twenty-first birthday. In everything he did he strove to maximise certainty and minimise surprises, firmly believing that careful preparation was the best guarantee of success. He was aware that fussing over details, when he should be delegating and focusing on the "big picture", was considered a weakness in a person of his seniority. But he'd learnt from bitter experience that people 'do what's checked, not what you expect' - a maxim he'd adopted from an American management guru. He was adamant that scrupulous attention to detail had got him where he was today: the CEO of a large corporation.

The hotel was a vast Victorian building perched on a cliff top with magnificent views over the Atlantic. The old timber window frames - hundreds of them - that used to rattle when the wind was in the west, had been replaced with white PVC triple-glazed units. Now the screeching of the seagulls swooping and wheeling outside could barely be heard, as if they had been fitted with invisible silencers. The hotel's expansive roof had been retiled and some of the redundant chimney stacks, turrets and finials had been swept away. Black solar panels had been fitted to the south facing elevations. A neon sign brazenly announced 'Westcliff Hotel' in large illuminated blue letters. Sir Cedric, a traditionalist and wary of changes for change's sake, wasn't at all sure that he approved.

As he alighted from his chauffeur driven car, Sir Cedric was surprised to hear music. He paused to listen and traced the sound to the concrete bollards lining the approach to the hotel entrance. On closer examination, he spotted speakers cunningly installed in each bollard. He shook his head in disbelief. Glass doors opened magically and he found himself in a vast reception area that reminded him of a Bavarian castle. A huge stone fireplace dominated one wall, culminating in a domed ceiling decorated with shooting stars, picked out in gold leaf. A gigantic chandelier, encrusted with bright red and blue pieces of glass, hung from the ceiling. The wall behind the reception desk wasn't a wall at all, but an aquarium. A constant stream of bubbles rose up to the surface, like sparkling wine in a flute. Colourful, translucent fish darted through bright green foliage and nosed their way through a network of valleys and caves. King Ludwig II would have felt completely at home.

'Goodness,' said Sir Cedric to his chauffeur, 'I've been coming here for years. The place is hardly recognisable.'

True to form, it was Sir Cedric's habit to check into the hotel the night before annual awaydays. It provided him with the opportunity to collect his thoughts and make last minute preparations: to have a final read-through of the documentation, to put the finishing touches to his opening speech, to double check the times for breaks and the arrangements for lunch.

He decided to inspect the conference room they'd been allocated. The events manager, a well-groomed young woman in a navy blue uniform with a colourful cravat, accompanied him. She stooped to swipe the door handle with a plastic card, pushed a strand of hair back behind her ear, and switched on the lights.

Sir Cedric took one look. 'I'm afraid this will have to be reconfigured. It's too formal, much too formal. I don't want any tables, just the chairs arranged in a big U shape. And you can get rid of that podium. I certainly won't be needing that!'

'Certainly, Sir Cedric.' The events manager made a note on her clipboard.

'And this music,' he waved vaguely in the direction of the ceiling, 'we'll obviously need to have that switched off.'

'Of course. No problem, Sir Cedric.' She made another note.

He returned to his suite on the top floor, resplendent with a jacuzzi and four poster king-sized bed. He gently squeezed a plum in the fruit bowl to check that it was ripe, poured himself a glass of champagne and phoned his wife. 'Pity you aren't with me, dear. The hotel has to be seen to be believed. Totally transformed. God knows what the refurbishment must have cost.'

Next morning, Sir Cedric rose early, swam a couple of lengths of the hotel pool, spent ten minutes in the sauna, took a shower, dressed in one of his immaculate suits and, over a light breakfast, read through his welcoming speech one last time. He changed a few words here and there with his fountain pen and, precisely half an hour before the awayday was due to start, he went to the anteroom where he mingled with the directors as they arrived and were offered coffee and croissants. Sir Cedric was accomplished at small talk, circulating effortlessly, welcoming everybody and putting them at their ease.

When the time came for the formal proceedings to begin, the participants moved obediently through into the conference room. Sir Cedric was pleased to see that the desks had disappeared but alarmed to find music was still playing. He asked the HR director to summon the events manager and, while they waited for her to arrive, some directors, keen to be seen to take the initiative, experimented with various switches. Lights came on and off, curtains closed with a gentle hum and opened again, a huge screen descended from the ceiling, hovered momentarily, and rose majestically back up into its casing. A glitterball turned slowly on its axis, scattering lights like confetti into every corner of the room.

But the music played on.

The events manager, still clutching her clipboard, arrived and joined the hunt to locate the elusive switch that would silence the music. Looking increasingly flustered, with escaped strands of hair dangling over her glasses, she eventually admitted defeat. 'I do apologise. I'll put out a call for maintenance.'

A man arrived dressed in overalls, pulling a trolley with a tool box. 'Since the refurbishment we've been having a few teething problems.' He gave Sir Cedric a disconcerting wink, as if to acknowledge him as an accomplice who surely understood such things. 'I've just checked the wiring diagram and it would seem that no switches have been installed to isolate the sound system in any of the meeting rooms. I'll have to open up some ceiling panels and disconnect the speakers.' Another wink.

'Are you serious?' said Sir Cedric. 'We obviously can't conduct our business with this din going on.'

'Don't worry, we'll get it sorted,' said the events manager, as much to reassure herself as anyone else. 'In the meantime, I'll get the music turned off at the central panel.'

'Yes please,' said Sir Cedric, feeling irritated but remaining outwardly calm. 'We need to make a start. We are losing valuable time.'

But the music continued, if anything a little louder.

'Ladies and gentlemen,' Sir Cedric announced. 'I'm afraid we need to take a short break while we wait for this music to be turned off. Please be back here in ten minutes.'

Sir Cedric was not at all pleased. He was a stickler for punctuality and they were already running late. What's more, the music was inane, some sort of jangly pop music, a far cry from the soothing Baroque music he much preferred. Just two weeks previously he'd been at Glyndebourne enjoying Handel's *Giulio Cesare*. Reluctantly, he pushed the memory aside and, recalling Wellington's advice, 'wise men pee when they can, fools pee when they must', took the opportunity to pop to the loo.

He swept into what had always been the gents and found himself in a room painted in subtle shades of pink, with cubicles and no urinals. 'They've gone way over the top in here,' he muttered to himself as he used a toilet in one of the cubicles. It was only when he emerged at exactly the same time as an elderly woman from an adjoining cubicle that the truth dawned on him. 'I'm so sorry, madam, please forgive me. I've been coming here for years and this has always been the gents.' The woman looked far from convinced and he made a quick exit, bumping into the events manager as she scurried back to the conference room.

'Whose idea was it to change the toilets around?' he asked. 'For as long as I can remember this has always been the gents. Almost as silly as having music you can't switch off.'

'I think you'll find everything is in order now, Sir Cedric. The music in the hotel has been temporarily silenced and during your lunch break I've arranged for the maintenance team to disconnect the speakers in your conference room.'

'Why bother? Just leave the music switched off. I'm sure none of your guests will mind.'

'Forgive me, Sir Cedric, but we need to restore the music to the communal areas as soon as possible. It's company policy. Research has shown that music relaxes our guests and increases the productivity of our employees.'

Dumfounded, Sir Cedric, not for the first time, shook his head in disbelief. 'Well, so long as we can't hear it in the conference room.'

The morning's business was conducted without further mishap and, as they left the conference room for lunch, men in overalls, equipped with step-ladders, moved in and proceeded to remove ceiling panels. Some of the panels split and bits of polystyrene fluttered down like snowflakes to settle daintily on Sir Cedric's notes.

In the dining room, just as Sir Cedric and his team were enjoying their desserts, the music suddenly resumed, if anything more intrusively than before.

'I sincerely hope this means they've managed to disconnect the speakers in the conference room', said Sir Cedric to the HR director sitting on his immediate right. 'What a farce! By the way, what is this blasted tune? I can't get it out of my head.'

'I'm not sure. It's certainly catchy.'

Sir Cedric turned to the IT director seated on his left. 'Reuben, you're a young chap, do you happen to know what this tune is? I can't place it. It's driving me mad.'

Reuben cocked his head. 'It's vaguely familiar, but I can't think what it's called. They've played it a few times and I've been it humming ever since.'

In desperation, Sir Cedric beckoned to a passing waitress. 'This tune,' he looked up at the dining room ceiling, 'would you happen to know what it is?'

The waitress inclined her head and listened. Suddenly she beamed. 'Yes sir. It's an instrumental version of Joe Dolce's hit, Shaddapya Face.'

Back at the office after the awayday, Cedric's PA asked him how it had gone.

'Eventful would be a fair description.'

'And how did you find the hotel?'

'Interesting,' he replied. 'Never a dull moment.'

'What's that tune you're humming?' she asked.

'I'm surprised you don't know it,' said Sir Cedric with a straight face. 'I'm reliably informed it's called Shaddapya Face. Catchy isn't it?'

The Experiment

Dennis gave a whoop of joy when his wife, Alice, told him she was pregnant.

'Wow, that's great! Really great.' He gave Alice a big hug. 'It means we'll have the wherewithal to conduct that experiment.'

'What?' said Alice, pulling away, somewhat taken aback. 'How can you possibly think of our baby as a wherewithal? Sounds like something from *The Importance of Being Earnest*.'

Dennis giggled, appreciating his wife's wit. 'Ah, in a handbag! Sorry, darling, I didn't mean it to sound at all like that.'

'Anyway,' Alice continued, 'I'm surprised you're prepared to contemplate experimenting with our own baby. Mightn't it be chancy?'

'Chancy? Surely you don't really think it would be risky.' Dennis cupped both her hands in his. He loved her hands, so smooth with long, elegant fingers. 'If I remember rightly, you were happy enough to carry out the experiment using someone else's baby.'

'Yes, but that was different. It wasn't my baby, sorry, *our* baby. Anyway, you'll recall there were no takers even though we offered a fee. No one was daft enough to risk it.'

'Well, there's no rush. We've a few months to think about it, take advice and weigh up the risks before deciding whether or not to go ahead.'

Dennis encased Alice in a long, lingering embrace as if he were worried she might escape. Alice rested her head against his shoulder.

'Sorry,' he whispered, 'it was clumsy of me to mention it. Let's just rejoice in the good news and think about it later. If you're really worried then of course there's no way we'll go ahead. We'll just forget the whole thing.'

But they didn't forget. As Alice's bump grew, he/she was nicknamed 'Withal', a private joke that mystified everyone except the happy couple.

Both Alice and Dennis were research graduates at a large pharmaceutical company. Their place of work was a cross between a modern redbrick university and a concentration camp: extensive modern buildings in a rural setting, surrounded by a high perimeter fence to deter animal rights protesters. Security was always tight with two different gatehouses where passes were checked and numerous barriers had to be navigated. During the COVID pandemic a skeleton staff, Alice and Dennis amongst them, lived onsite to care for the hapless monkeys, rabbits, rats and mice.

It was during this idyllic period, living in a carefree bubble with like-minded colleagues, that Dennis had shown Alice an article in a psychological journal speculating about the likely adverse effects on child development of lockdown, particularly of mask-wearing. The article, called '*Face Masks: The potential negative short-term and long-term effects for newborn babies deprived of normal face-to-face interactions'*, suggested that the wearing of masks by caregivers, 'might potentially delay the baby's neurodevelopment and the bonding that takes place between baby and parent'. The article predicted that mask-wearing would hamper reciprocal interactions between a baby and his/her parents and, in particular, that smiling, normally occurring at approximately six weeks of age, would in all probability be severely delayed.

Dennis had always been interested in the so-called nature-nurture debate. Having read widely on the subject, including Steven Pinker's *'The Blank State: The Modern Denial of Human Nature'*, he was persuaded that most human behaviour traits were attributable to genetical pre-wiring and other biological factors. This, Dennis maintained, almost certainly included smiling. He maintained that babies smiled at approximately six weeks of age, not because it had taken them six weeks to learn to smile, but because it took that long for facial muscles to develop and become capable of producing a social smile, known technically as a Duchenne smile. Wind, since it was involuntary, didn't count.

The majority of Dennis's colleagues at the laboratory were environmentalists, arguing that babies had to learn to smile and that this normally took six weeks. Dennis was keen to prove them wrong by conducting an experiment that, for ethical reasons, no one had previously dared to undertake.

The experiment was simple. For the first six weeks of the baby's life, everyone who came into contact with the newborn would be required to wear a skin-coloured mask that covered the whole face, with small holes for seeing and breathing. After exactly six weeks mask wearing would be discontinued and, if the baby smiled, it would suggest that smiling was an inborn trait. If, on the other hand, smiling was absent, and took additional weeks to occur, it would suggest that smiling was a learnt behaviour, i.e. was attributable to nurture not nature.

During the first few months of Alice's pregnancy, Dennis conducted a gentle campaign designed to overcome Alice's understandable reluctance.

'What harm do you think it could do? It's not really risky like the Little Albert Experiment with rats and loud noises. At worst, Withal's smile might be delayed for a few weeks while he (Dennis was convinced the baby was a he) catches up.'

'Yes, but you can't predict what else might be affected. Smiling at six weeks might be associated with lots of other developmental building blocks.'

'Such as?'

'I don't know! Perhaps he'll be emotionally retarded in ways we can't predict.'

'My guess is that it will do no harm,' said Dennis, doing his best to be reassuring, but conscious that he had no hard data to back up this assertion.

'Yes, but that's just a guess.'

'Just think,' said Dennis, changing his tack, 'we'll be able to write it up and have a paper published. It's likely to receive widespread attention. It'll be referenced in all the journals, we'll have a Wikipedia entry, we'll be famous. You never know what it might lead to.'

'Perhaps it'll give your career a boost. I'll just be a mum stuck at home with a retarded baby.'

One day Alice's parents called in, en route to their place in Spain. Their visits were rare since they lived 200 miles away in

Hartlepool. Alice's dad was a self-made timber merchant, seeking to sell his company and retire on the proceeds. They were understandably delighted to be expecting their first grandchild and Alice's mother offered to come and stay for a couple of weeks to help out after the baby had been born.

'Thanks, mum, that would be very helpful,' said Alice. 'But you might have to wear a mask.'

'Why's that, dear? Worried about COVID?'

'No, it's because Dennis is keen to conduct an experiment.'

'An experiment?' Alice's father chipped in. 'What sort of experiment?'

Alice explained the gist of the idea, knowing that trying to fascinate them about Duchenne smiles and the nature-nurture debate was as futile as trying to convince a Jehovah's Witness that blood transfusions were a good idea.

'That's bananas, absolutely bonkers!' Alice's father shouted. 'Surely you're not going to agree to that?'

'Dennis is very keen to go ahead,' Alice said defensively. 'It's never been done before and it would attract a lot of attention.'

'You bet it would. I should think it'll get you bloody well locked up. Crazy, absolutely crazy!'

'Calm down, dear,' said Alice's mother, putting a restraining hand on her husband's arm. 'I'm sure Dennis knows what he's doing.' She'd always been in awe of her son-in-law's intellect, convinced he'd been a good catch.

'Oh yeah, since when? He works in a lab with bloody monkeys. What the hell does he know about babies?'

That night, snuggled up in bed, with Dennis's hand resting gently on her tummy feeling the baby moving, Alice suddenly announced, 'Let's go ahead with the experiment.'

Dennis sat bolt upright and looked into Alice's eyes. 'Really? Why the sudden change of heart? I'd pretty well given up on the idea.'

'Two reasons. First, because I know it means a lot to you and I can see it would attract widespread attention. Secondly, because my father is dead set against it. I've always kowtowed to his wishes and I've decided it's high time I stood up to him.'

'Are you sure?' I don't want you to go ahead just to please me or to annoy him.'

'No, I've done a lot of reading around the subject and I've given it a lot of thought. I'm as sure as I can be that there won't be any lasting adverse consequences. I definitely want us to do it.'

Dennis gave her a kiss on both cheeks. 'Well, that's terrific, but only if you're quite sure. We can pull the plug at any time if you get worried. You must promise to tell me if you want to stop.'

And so they went ahead. Alice gave birth to a healthy baby girl at home with no complications and a chatty midwife in attendance. The baby was now called Sarah rather than Withal, and Dennis took paternity leave on full pay to supervise the experiment, in particular to check that no one cheated by removing their mask. Despite misgivings, everyone who came into contact with baby Sarah, including the health visitor and various neighbours, dutifully wore their flesh-coloured masks. Alice's mother was the only person Dennis trusted to spend time with the baby unsupervised. Alice's father refused point blank to visit until the mask wearing 'nonsense' was over.

As the end of the six week period of compulsory mask-wearing drew near, excitement mounted. Would Sarah smile or not?

Dennis wrote a paper about the experiment with, like Boris Johnson writing his pro and anti-Brexit speeches, two different outcomes. Laboratory colleagues of Dennis's laid bets. A reporter at the local newspaper got wind of the experiment and wrote a column with the headline, 'Charles Darwin, right or wrong?' The national news picked up the story and reporters and cameramen congregated outside Alice and Dennis's house, much to the annoyance of their neighbours. Dennis gave door-step interviews and photographs were taken of him wearing his mask giving a thumbs-up sign. A photographer from *The Sun* attempted to climb a drainpipe at the back of the house and take a sneaky shot of Sarah in her cot. The health visitor admitted she'd been offered a bribe to invalidate the experiment by taking off her mask and smiling at the baby. A small group of hostile protesters joined the press pack waving homemade banners saying, 'Babies have rights too', 'Smile baby, smile', and 'Criminals wear masks'.

Finally the day for masks to be removed arrived. An independent witness from *Psychology Today* was in attendance together with the BBC's science correspondent and a camera-man. Alice, Dennis, and Alice's mother ceremonially removed their masks. Alice picked up baby Sarah, gazed into her eyes and gave her a beautiful, loving smile. After an agonising minute or so, Sarah looked at Alice's mother and smiled at her. Alice burst into tears; tears of relief.

When, at last, Alice's father visited to meet his granddaughter, he was unrepentant. 'Of course,' he declared, 'I could have told you all along that the poor little blighter would smile.'

'Oh, how's that?' asked Dennis.

'And it's got nothing to do with your nature-nurture garbage.'

'Really? Go on,' said Dennis, attempting to humour his father-in-law.

'Yep, it's simple. It's because she thought you all looked bloody stupid wearing those damn silly masks.'

Alice's mother looked on, smiling quietly to herself.

The Anti-Climax

I spotted him by sheer chance. There he was, all alone, having a late breakfast in Fortnum & Mason, sitting at the corner table Adam Faith used to use as his office. I'd recognised him straightaway, eyes twinkling with wry amusement at the state of the world, grey hair cut short, wearing a grey suit and a black open neck shirt. It was definitely him or, if not, a damn good lookalike. I'd seen him performing at the O2 Arena a year or so ago and been amazed that at his age he could manage 27 songs without faltering and skip on and off the stage like a gazelle.

Actually, I have a knack for bumping into famous people quite by chance. Once in a restaurant my wife and I happened to be sitting at the table next to Judy Dench and her daughter. Then there was the time on holiday in Yorkshire when we exchanged a few words with Alan Bennett in a teashop. I'd recently read *The Uncommon Reader* and told him how much I'd enjoyed it, especially the bit about the Queen having her favourite book hidden behind cushions in the Gold State Coach.

I once met John Cleese walking along a road in Notting Hill, and no, he wasn't doing a funny walk. Who else? Spike Milligan in Finchley. He was looking glum (I didn't tell him that I thought he looked ill) so I tried to cheer him up. I told him how I was a fan of the Goon Show in the good old days. But he looked even sadder and went off muttering, 'Ying tong, ying tong, ying tong, yiddle I po'. Then there was Johnathan Miller near Covent Garden. I'd loved his production of *La Traviata* - my favourite opera. I told him that Mimi's death scene was the best one I'd ever seen. Oh, and Ian McEwan in, of all places, Blackwell's in Oxford. I told him I'd read all his books and asked him when the next one was coming out and why he was loitering in a bookshop and not at home writing.

The list goes on. You'll be thinking I'm a name dropper, which is fair enough, I suppose.

Way back, I even met Laurence Olivier and Vivien Leigh when they lived in Oxfordshire. My aunt was an estate agent at the time and they were putting their house on the market and she'd gone to take particulars and measure up. I held one end of the tape measure for her. The Oliviers gave us a cup of tea. I was only a teenager at the time so I chatted away happily, not really appreciating how famous they were.

I always make a point of talking to the famous people I meet. My wife worries that they'll find it intrusive but I think, what the hell, they can tell me to piss off if they want to. Lightning isn't likely to strike in the same place twice is it? If I don't talk to them while I have the opportunity I'll surely live to regret it.

Anyway, just about all of them seem happy to be recognised and to have a brief chat. I'm always very polite and appreciative of their achievements, thanking them for the pleasure they've given me, and so on. There have been a couple of people who've been a bit shirty but I'd best not name them. The worst was Jimmy Saville (I guess it's OK to name baddies?). Mind you, I'd no idea he was a baddie at the time - none of us did - even though he seemed a bit creepy. I bumped into him in Manchester after a university rave-up where he'd been the DJ. Well, to be honest, I didn't exactly bump into him because I was deliberately waiting by his Rolls Royce. I was a spotty youth at the time so I suppose he didn't fancy me. A bit of an insult really since, as we learnt later, he didn't seem very choosy. I asked him if I could interview him for the university rag and he told me to bugger off. I remember being surprised at the amount of blue smoke that came out of his exhaust pipes as he accelerated away. I reckoned it was in need of a service. A bit of a laugh really, him in a Rolls that needed new piston rings.

Meeting the Archbishop of Canterbury in Canterbury Cathedral was a bit of a hoot. I asked him what he was doing in Canterbury when he lived in London. He chuckled and said that putting in an occasional appearance at Canterbury was in the job description. I told him I loved the vaulted ceiling, and he was kind enough to pretend he'd never noticed it before. I was tempted to ask him if he believed in God, but I didn't because I thought it would be a leading question, perhaps the *ultimate* leading question! He could hardly say he didn't could he, even if it were true?

Of course, I've made some embarrassing mistakes. I once met a man in Maidenhead High Street who looked very familiar and I greeted him like a long-lost friend, all the while racking my brains trying to work out how I knew him. He was very polite and said, 'Hello, nice to see you.' He might even have said 'again', but I can't be sure. It was only after we'd parted that it suddenly dawned on me who it was: Terry Wogan. And there have been some missed opportunities. I once saw Paddy Ashdown walking along The Strand (actually, being ex-military, he was doing something akin to a brisk march rather than a walk). Anyway, I knew I knew him but it was only after we had passed that I worked out who he was. Chasing after him wouldn't have been dignified and, at the pace he was moving, I mightn't have caught up with him. Still, I'd liked to have shaken his hand and told him I'd been voting Lib Dem for years, alas, to no avail.

Who else?

Generally speaking, politicians are more elusive - quite understandably when you consider the flack they get. Of course, they are 'out and about' in the run up to elections (mostly on doorsteps if reports are to be believed) but otherwise they are nowhere to be seen except on the telly making empty promises. Meeting Douglas Hurd when he was Foreign Secretary was a complete fluke. I was sitting on a wooden bench watching my young son play in a school cricket match when he happened along and sat down on the same bench. Even asked me if I minded if he sat there! A charming bloke, not at all like a politician. I tried not to spoil his afternoon by asking him questions about foreign policy, but I did enquire where his security blokes were. He said they were back in the carpark waiting by his official car. I said, 'shouldn't they have checked me out before they let you sit down beside me?' He laughed and said I looked harmless enough. I've often wondered since whether that was a compliment.

Joanna Lumley - how could I forget meeting her? I was

walking along the South Bank one summer's evening. It was dusk and there she was gazing across the Thames at the spot where the Garden Bridge was going to be built. The trees on that stretch of the Embankment all had bright yellow notices tied to their trunks by protesters saying 'Save this Tree!' Lots of them - maybe a dozen or more. I asked her whether she felt safe, there all on her own with it starting to get dark. She told me her chauffeur was nearby but I couldn't see him. Of course, her husky voice is famous but I thought it sounded a bit affected. I didn't say anything about the irony of having to cut down lots of trees in order to build a bridge with trees on it. Cowardly, but there you are. I try to avoid controversy. Still, the bridge never happened so it all ended well.

If I put my mind to it, there are probably other famous people I've met but surely that's enough. I did warn you I'm a name-dropper!

Anyway, I was going to tell you about my chance meeting with Leonard Cohen in Fortnum & Mason. I've been a fan of his since the 70's, so seeing him sitting there all alone was a special moment, and I mean SPECIAL. To say I'm a fan is a massive understatement. Truth is I'm in total awe of the man and know most of his haunting lyrics by heart.

I went over to his table and said, 'Excuse me, Mr Cohen, but may I thank you for all the pleasure you've given me over many years.'

He gave a self-deprecating smile and replied, 'Most kind. You sure know how to humour an old man.'

'Not at all,' I replied. 'I was at your concert at the 02 Arena last year. Unforgettable!'

'Too kind,' he repeated.

'Far from it. I must say, I can't help being glad that your manager stole all your money while you were away in that monastery. Your loss was certainly our gain.'

He sighed. 'Yes, if I'd still had my money, I guess I'd never have embarked on those world tours.'

'Sorry, you must have been asked this many times before, but how do you manage to think of all those haunting lyrics? You must be a lateral thinker.'

He gave an enigmatic smile. 'I carry a notebook with me and jot things down.'

'Gosh, have you got it with you now?'

'Yes, I'm never without.'

'I know it's cheeky, but could you give me an example of an entry?'

I must break off here to emphasise the sheer genius of many of Cohen's lyrics. So many examples:

'You touched her perfect body with your mind.'
'There's a crack in everything.'
'Dance me through the panic 'til I'm safely gathered in.'
'I ache in the places where I used to play.'
'My heart the shape of a begging bowl.'
'A thousand kisses deep.'

He reached into his inside pocket and brought out a small notebook and flicked it open. In a deadpan voice (oh, that voice!) he read: 'Woke at 6.30. Had a pee. Let the cat out. Took my medication. Had a black coffee.'

I said, 'Oh, is that it? I must admit I was expecting something more profound.'

'Nope, that's it,' and he shut his notebook with a snap.

I still don't know if he was taking the mickey.

The Wedding Anniversary

It was a surprise. Sir Richard and Lady Elinger's four children, all accomplished in their own fields, had clubbed together and arranged for them to celebrate their 60th wedding anniversary at Milton Court, a manor house hotel in the Cotswolds with Three Michelin Stars. The hotel's strap-line was 'Beyond Excellent, Beyond Sublime'.

The children (two sons, two daughters) had organised everything down to the last detail: a Mercedes to convey their elderly parents to the hotel in style (a journey of 62 miles), a suite with a sitting room, a huge bedroom with a king-sized four-poster bed, and a luxurious marble bathroom with gold-plated taps. In addition, the following items were to be placed on a highly polished round-table in the sitting room: a generous bouquet of flowers, a home-made lemon drizzle cake, a bowl of fresh fruit, a bottle of Glenkinchie 12 Year Old Single Malt Scotch Whisky (Sir Richard's favourite tipple), a bottle of Harvey's Amontillado Sherry (Penelope's favourite tipple), and two glass bottles of spring water.

Milton Court was approached along an immaculate avenue

lined with whimsical topiary. The building, of honey-coloured stone, was vast, with many gables, mullioned widows and a forest of chimney stacks. The date 1633 was carved in stone above the front entrance. A huge cedar tree stood proudly at the west end of the building and, beyond that, the River Windrush flowed swiftly by, with trout nosing their way against the current. The hotel's grounds were impeccable, with numerous paved pathways, a small lake, a Japanese garden, a croquet lawn, a well-stocked kitchen garden and a vast expanse of greenhouses. The whole place reeked of opulence. You could not fail to be impressed.

The Elinger's Mercedes drew up, the tyres crunching deliciously on the gravel, during a sudden April shower and two porters with umbrellas dashed out to greet them. Sir Richard and Penelope alighted from the back seat, struggling slightly, while a third porter lifted their cases out of the boot. Short of having a guard of honour, it was as if royalty had arrived. They were an elegant couple, tall and thin, only slightly stooped. Penelope took great pride in her hair - long and grey and swept up into a chignon. A receptionist, a charming young woman called Dawn, greeted them by name and escorted them to the lounge where, while sitting on a generous sofa with ample cushions, they were offered a welcoming glass of champagne and a bowl of olives.

'Thank you,' beamed Sir Richard, 'start as you mean to go on, I say.' Penelope, fussing with the cushions, declined champagne, opting instead for a glass of filtered tap water.

'When you're ready, I'll show you to your room,' said Dawn. 'You are in one of the honeymoon suites with fine views over the garden.'

'Our honeymoon was sixty years ago,' Penelope said wistfully. 'I assume our luggage has preceded us?'

'Of course, Lady Elinger,' Dawn replied reassuringly. 'Take your time, everything is in hand. Just let me know when you're ready to be shown to your suite.'

They sat in silence for a while, recovering from their journey, Sir Richard with his eyes shut and Penelope flicking through the glossy pages of *Country Life*. There were two other couples in the spacious lounge: a man with a large stomach accompanied by a black woman wearing bangles and beads and a brightly coloured dress, and a young couple, smiling coyly at each other. Nobody spoke. They just sat there reverentially, sipping champagne, with piano music - it sounded like Mozart - playing softly from concealed speakers. A waiter hovered in one corner, occasionally busying himself by plumping up cushions and needlessly rearranging the mustard-coloured window drapes.

The Elinger's suite, on the first floor, looking south across the croquet lawn, was sumptuous. Dawn briefed them on how to unlock and lock their door, how to use the remote control for the TV, which light switches worked which lights, how to connect to the hotel's Wi-Fi, where to charge their phones and how to use the coffee percolator.

'Oh dear,' said Penelope. 'I hope we can remember all that.'

'Don't hesitate to ask if there is anything you need, anything at all. Just phone Reception,' Dawn smiled, moving gracefully across the plush carpet towards the door.

Sir Richard and Penelope unpacked their cases, hanging their clothes in the generous 'his and her' wardrobes and putting their toilet bags in the marble bathroom with 'his and her' wash basins. Penelope, conscious as ever about the need to save the planet, tut-tutted at the proliferation of large, white, fluffy bath towels.

By the time they had unpacked, the rain had stopped and the gardens were bathed in sunshine. 'Let's have a look around,' suggested Penelope. 'It would be good to stretch our legs after the drive.' Donning raincoats and armed with a furled umbrella just in case, they stepped out into the April sunshine. As they passed the croquet lawn, Sir Richard, a keen croquet player, muttered to himself about the wrong sort of hoops, wire instead of iron. Penelope sighed, having heard the same complaint many times on their annual visits to Glyndebourne.

The stepping stones in the Japanese garden were an unexpected challenge for the elderly couple, with Penelope losing her footing at one stage, only saving herself from a fall by grabbing her husband. They clung together momentarily, swaying like an old wooden fence in a breeze.

'Surely there should be a warning notice, these steps are perilous,' said Penelope. 'I shall tell them about it.'

'I'm sure you will, dear,' said Sir Richard, compliant as ever.

Safely back in their room, Sir Richard decided to take a shower before changing for dinner.

'Wait a moment, Dickie, you'll need a nonslip mat. That marble floor will be treacherous once it gets wet.' They searched all the likely places where a mat might be stored: the wardrobes, the bedside cupboards, under the wash basins, beside the bidet. All to no avail.

'Very remiss of them not to provide a nonslip mat,' grumbled Penelope. 'I'll phone Reception.'

The receptionist, a different one, Dawn had gone off duty, sounded puzzled. 'Certainly, madam. I'll arrange for one to be delivered immediately.' And sure enough, after a short wait, a man called Stuart arrived with a rolled-up mat, carrying it as if it was a crown on a cushion. 'Apologies. Are you sure there isn't a nonslip mat on the shelf behind the bath taps?'

'Well, we've looked everywhere,' said Penelope indignantly.

'May I check, madam? If there isn't a mat, I'll need to alert room service.'

Stuart stepped into the bathroom and, unfurling a towel with a flourish, revealed a nonslip mat.

'How extraordinary!' said Penelope. 'I've never seen a mat disguised as a towel before.'

With both mats safely installed, Sir Richard showered without mishap, relishing the enthusiasm of the rainforest showerhead.

Dressed, Penelope in a flowing turquoise dress and Sir Richard in a dark suit with a colourful tie, they locked their room and went to the dining room, a large conservatory with views of floodlit statues on the terrace beyond. A dozen or so couples were already seated, including the people they had seen in the lounge. A waiter, with a heavy French accent, fussed over them, installing starched white napkins on their laps and, as if he'd never done it before, explaining the 7-course taster menu they were about to explore and the selection of classic wines that would accompany each course.

'No idea what any of that meant,' grumbled Sir Richard cheerfully, adjusting his hearing aids.

'Just sit back and enjoy it, dear,' Penelope replied.

They had just finished their fourth course, Cornish crab ravioli with a courgette and lemongrass bisque, when another couple were ushered past them. The man, tall and distinguished, with a well-trimmed grey beard, suddenly paused. 'Good God, is that you Penelope?'

Penelope looked up. Her mouth dropped open. 'Arnold?'

'It *is* you! Well, I'll be damned! How long has it been? Forty years? More?'

Penelope, fell slowly forward, her head narrowly missing a wine glass and her arm sending a plate crashing to the floor. There was a shocked silence, with Sir Richard momentarily frozen, before guests at nearby tables gasped and waiters rushed to help.

A&E in Cheltenham General were very thorough. They insisted on giving Penelope a scan to check that she hadn't had a TIA. In a curtained cubicle, waiting for the verdict and to have the cut on her forehead stitched, Sir Richard popped the inevitable question.

'What on earth happened? Who was that fellow who recognised you? An old work colleague?'

'Yes, dear, you could say that. I haven't seen him for as long as I can remember. Seeing him again was quite a shock.'

'Obviously. I've never seen you in such a state.'

'Yes, dear, he's someone I don't want to see again. I'm afraid I can't go back to the hotel. I'm sorry to spoil our anniversary, but we'll have to go home.'

And so, in the early hours of the morning, a taxi was called to convey Sir Richard and his wife home. During the journey, their driver occasionally glanced at the elderly couple in his mirror and assumed they were dozing. But Sir Richard was busy speculating about the significance of Arnold, and Penelope was busy worrying about what she would say to her children.

Later that day, a chauffeur from Milton Court delivered their luggage. It was exquisitely packed and was accompanied by a huge basket of flowers and a 'get well' card signed by the staff. Cunningly concealed inside a large, fluffy, white towel, was a nonslip mat.

The Sailor

I didn't appreciate being treated as a suspect even though I knew it was standard procedure.

'So, it's normal for him to disappear for three weeks without you knowing his precise whereabouts?' The young policeman - he didn't look much older than my son - clearly didn't consider it in the least normal.

'Yes, as I've already told you, we have an understanding. It's an amicable arrangement. I hate sailing, he loves it, so I go on holiday doing my own thing while he goes sailing doing his. We go our separate ways for a few weeks every summer. Been doing it for years.'

'And on previous occasions he has always returned as planned, when he said he would?'

'Yes, he's a very organised man, a stickler for punctuality. It's completely out of character for Mark to be late back.'

'Hmm,' said the young man, looking doubtful, seemingly at a loss to know what to make of a married couple having separate holidays. His companion, a young woman, chipped in, 'Would you say your husband is trustworthy?'

'That's an odd question, what are you implying? Anyway, the answer is yes, totally trustworthy. We've been happily married for 32 years.'

Thankfully, after taking numerous details and a photograph I gave them of Mark on his sailing boat, they closed their notebooks and promised to keep me informed as their enquiries proceeded.

'You will of course let us know if your husband turns up or contacts you.' I assured them I would.

But I'm getting ahead of myself.

I had called the police after Mark failed to return from his sailing trip as planned. It wasn't like him not to let me know if he was going to be late. Initially I wasn't concerned. I just thought he'd been held up by bad weather, or even a traffic jam on the journey back from Portsmouth. Anyway, I was busy opening up the house and unpacking after my trip to Pompei and Herculaneum.

I tried Mark's mobile a number of times and left messages on his voice mail. The last time we'd spoken was when he phoned after his first week to say all was going well. He had docked at a marina in Guernsey and was loading up with supplies. He sounded perfectly happy, said the weather had been kind and that everything was going according to plan. He was confident that, unless unexpectedly becalmed, he'd be safely back in Portsmouth in a couple of weeks' time.

Then nothing. It was totally out of character.

After a sleepless night I started to ring round to see if Mark had been in touch with anyone else. I phoned our son and daughter, both recently married and busy with their own lives, to see if their father had contacted them. As I expected, neither had heard anything. I phoned Mark's office - he is a director at a large software house, here in Guildford - to see if his secretary had heard anything. Nothing. I phoned Mark's best friend, the one he regularly plays golf with. No, he'd had no contact with Mark since he left and was looking forward to the game they had arranged for Wednesday. Geoff, bless him, phoned quite often, offering to come round. I said no, best to keep clear, Mark could show up at any time.

After a couple of days, increasingly convinced something was seriously amiss, I rang the police and reported Mark missing.

Five more days went by; slow days with me in limbo unable to settle into anything. I gave myself projects to keep busy. I spring cleaned the house, took some bin bags to the local dump, took books to the local Oxfam shop. Neighbours popped in to ask if there was anything they could do to help. My son offered to come and stay so that I had 'a man in the house'. Various friends rang to check I was OK and ask if I'd heard anything. But, even though I appreciated everyone's kindness, it all seemed quite futile.

Then the police rang to say there had been a development. Could they come round? It sounded ominous. I asked them why they couldn't tell me there and then on the phone, but they insisted it would be best if they told me in person.

As before, two officers came, older and more senior than before. We sat in the kitchen. They looked rather solemn and, politely declining my offer of cups of tea, broke the news that Mark's yacht had been found drifting a few miles off Falmouth.

'The vessel has been retrieved by the coastguard. I'm sorry to tell you that they report it is partially submerged and severely damaged by fire. The cabin is totally burnt out and there is no sign of life.'

They left, as before, assuring me they'd keep me fully informed of any developments.

A few days later Mark's partially decomposed body was washed up on a Cornish beach ten miles west of Falmouth. His identity had to be confirmed by dental records. The police returned, looking business-like. They expressed their condolences and, somewhat sheepishly, asked if I'd mind answering a few more questions.

'Do you know this woman?' They produced a photograph of a dark-haired woman, middle-aged, smiling somewhat bashfully at the camera.

'No, I don't think so. She doesn't look familiar. Who is she?'

'You're quite sure you have never seen her before?'

I put my spectacles on and examined the photograph more closely. 'I'm confident I don't know her. Is she a colleague of Mark's?'

'It appears that she was rather more than a colleague. I'm sorry if this is upsetting news, but her badly burned body has been found washed up on the same stretch of shoreline as your late husband's. I'm afraid she was almost certainly on board your husband's yacht.'

I was incredulous. Upright, trustworthy Mark cheating on me? I never suspected. It didn't seem possible.

That evening Geoff came round to comfort me. He brought flowers and a bottle of wine. He was wearing the sandals he'd bought in Naples.

The Reader

It was completely unexpected, something he never thought he'd see.

For some obscure reason it reminded him of occasions when he'd expected to see something but hadn't. Like the time when he'd spent three days being driven along dusty tracks in the Kruger National Park, gazing into parched scrubland expecting to see a pride of lions, but none had appeared, only countless wildebeests and the occasional zebra. Or that time in an art gallery when he'd expected to see a painting by Albrecht Durer only to be confronted with a notice explaining it had been removed for restoration. Or when he'd visited St Thomas's Hospital expecting to see his friend who, an hour before, had been transferred to a hospice. Or when he'd gone to the cemetery, equipped with a bucket and scrubbing brush, ready to clean his great-grandfather's headstone, only to find it had been removed to make room for an extension to the church.

Why, he wondered, when suddenly confronted with something he'd never expected to see, was he reminded of things he had expected to see, but hadn't? He supposed it must be his mind playing silly tricks.

He blinked, half expecting the act of blinking to have rubbed her out. But there she was, conspicuous, not because of her oriental features, but because she was the only person reading a book. Everyone else, sitting opposite and on either side of her, sat gazing at the screens on their smart phones.

He'd spotted the distinctive cover immediately when, having settled in her seat, she'd produced the book from her rucksack. For a while it lay unopened on her lap as she scabbled around in the rucksack, eventually producing a pencil. Then, with what he thought was probably a sigh, she settled down to read, occasionally underlining a word and making a note in the margin.

He was taken aback because the chances of ever encountering anyone, let alone this young oriental woman, reading *that* book must be close to zero, perhaps even less than zero. He smiled to himself, appreciating that in terms of probability, less than zero was a mathematical impossibility.

The book had not been a success, long since remaindered and out of print. What, he wondered, was her interest in reading it and, even more intriguing, what was she jotting in the margins? He was too far away to see. Criticisms perhaps? Nothing she noted seemed expansive, just an occasional word here or there.

He considered his options: leave her to her labours or interrupt her? A binary choice, the former straightforward, the latter perilous and full of unknowns. Anyway, what could he possibly say that wouldn't seem banal or, even worse, patronising?

He recalled other occasions when he'd struggled to find the right words. The time, for example, when he'd been tongue-tied when Prince Philip demanded to know what the hell he was doing as the only bloke in a dance class - the implication being that he must be some sort of pervert. Or the time when he'd made a complete hash of asking his Pilates teacher, distractingly clad in a skin-tight leotard, out for a date. He wasn't sure she'd even twigged that's what he was doing. Or perhaps she had, but thought it kind to pretend she hadn't. Then there was that job interview when he was asked about his weaknesses. Totally thrown, he'd managed to mumble something about being indecisive. He didn't get the job, consoling himself that at least he'd been honest.

What could he say to the young woman? It was awkward. He'd have to get up and walk over to her, then stand while everyone else was seated. Should he bow or put his hands together in greeting? The situation wasn't conducive to having a quiet word. Everyone near her would inevitably overhear whatever he chose to say.

Suddenly she looked up, her pony-tail bobbing, and gazed out of the window. Fields flashed past. What was she thinking? Perhaps pondering something thought-provoking she'd just read? Or wondering whether it was worth continuing? Hard to tell. She looked at her wrist watch, gave a stifled yawn, wriggled in her seat, stretched her legs momentarily and then resumed her reading.

She looked a studious type. He wondered how old she was. Early thirties he guessed. Probably single, maybe a mature student or a professional person finding her way in life. But why *that* book? Pessimistically he assumed she must be reading it under sufferance, not voluntarily. A set text perhaps? Background reading before embarking on a project? And where, he wondered, had she acquired the book: from a library, from Amazon, perhaps a chance find in a charity shop? He longed to know.

He knew full well that he shouldn't be watching her like this, but he couldn't help it. He recalled the last time he'd got himself into a bit of bother on a train. He'd become mesmerised watching a young woman doing her eye makeup. He was quite convinced a sudden jolt would result in an accident, but somehow, swaying gracefully, she absorbed the jolts and continued to apply her mascara without mishap. Whilst he'd been lost in admiration, marvelling at her dexterity, she'd suddenly snapped shut her mirror, leant forward and told him to fuck off. He was so shocked that he couldn't think of anything to say in mitigation as she pointedly gathered up her things and moved to another seat.

Then there was that incident when a young, athletic black man had belligerently demanded to know why he was looking at him. The question came as a shock because, for once, he hadn't been looking, he'd merely glanced up as the young man sat down opposite him. Despite this, the young man had become increasingly agitated and repeated his question. When no answer was forthcoming, he'd leapt up with clenched fists and, dancing like Muhammad Ali, shouted, 'You're scared, man! Yeah man, shitting yourself aren't you?' before collapsing back into his seat guffawing with laughter.

He'd been seriously shaken by the incident, reflecting afterwards that he could easily have been mugged or stabbed.

The young woman rummaged in her rucksack again and fished out her smart phone, the book remaining open on her lap. She keyed in a word, looked thoughtful, then made another note in the margin of the book. He could hardly contain himself. What was she doing? What had she looked up? An obscure word perhaps? Probably something he could easily explain.

She turned down the corner of the page she'd been reading and closed the book. He didn't really approve of people who turned down corners, always preferring to use a book mark himself. Neither, for that matter, did he approve of people who annotated books. But he knew it would be churlish to reproach her.

The book lay on her lap and she leant back in her seat and closed her eyes.

He watched her. Had she stopped reading because she was bored, finding the book a hard slog? Perhaps she'd had a late night? He gazed at her and wondered.

Then, without warning, she stirred, opened her eyes and looked straight at him. Embarrassed, he immediately looked away, feigning disinterest. Had she sensed he was staring at her? Perhaps now was the moment to say something, to come clean, to allay her fears, maybe even offer to sign the book?

But, in the familiar grip of indecision, he did nothing, wrestling to suppress an overpowering urge to take another look, just a fleeting glance. He decided he'd permit himself to do so only after counting slowly to ten, a delaying tactic he'd employed to good effect on a number of previous occasions. But, he wondered, would that provide a long enough interval? To look up and find she was still looking at him would be impossibly embarrassing. In his confusion, he opted to busy himself cleaning his spectacles - a displacement activity that bought him a bit more time.

When eventually he dared to glance in her direction, there was a space where she had been. She'd gone!

He reflected ruefully that now he'd never know why she was reading that book and she would never know how close she'd come to meeting the author.

The Learning Curve

Mark was puzzled. After his first few weeks of callouts, despite emerging from his intensive training top of the class, feedback from his customers was disappointing. With a 5 star rating system, 5 being excellent and 1 being poor, customers consistently rated Mark no higher than a 3. Comments were optional, but when customers bothered to add something in the comments box, typically he was described as 'business-like, but with a tendency to be brusque and unfriendly'. This was especially puzzling because Mark was not a shy, retiring type and had always been popular at school and college.

'I'd best accompany you on a few callouts,' said Bert, his supervisor. 'We've got to get to the bottom of this.'

Mark, unmarried and in his late twenties, was a conscientious young man. He'd studied electronic engineering at college and been snapped up by Xerox once he'd qualified. He lived with his parents and a younger sister in Deptford and was saving towards a deposit to buy his own place. Once he had completed his training, learning how to service and repair big photocopying machines, he joined the team that responded to callouts in Central London.

True to his word, Bert accompanied him on a visit to the Stock Exchange. The plan was for Mark to stick to his normal routine while Bert observed without intervening. They presented their ID's at the reception desk and were directed to the fifth floor where they were met by a middle aged woman who looked relieved to see them. 'Sorry to have called you out. We've gone through the troubleshooting routine a couple of times but drawn a blank. Over to you.'

'No problem,' said Mark and opened up the copying machine to expose its innards, a mass of wires and connectors that looked like a telephone substation. The woman hovered, uncertain whether she should stay, while Mark set to work going through the diagnostic routine. Eventually, she said, 'Well, I'll leave you to it. My desk is just over there if you need me.'

'Thanks,' said Mark, gazing at flashing coloured lights on his computer. 'Shouldn't take us too long.'

Fifteen minutes later, Mark had successfully fixed the problem and run the machine through the testing routine to double-check that all was well. He went over to the where the woman was hunched over her computer screen.

'All done,' said Mark with a triumphant beam.

'Gosh,' she said, looking up. 'That didn't take long. Can you find your own way out?'

'Yep. Cheers,' said Mark.

Once outside, Bert suggested a chat over a cup of coffee.

'Tell me,' said Bert, 'was that typical or were you trying to impress me?'

'No, I did my best to forget you were there and carried on as normal. Did I do anything wrong?'

'Well,' said Bert, 'I think the problem is you were too efficient.'

'*Too efficient?* Surely you can never be too efficient?'

'What I mean is this. You did all the right things when it came to fixing the machine, that was certainly impressive. But you never established any sort of rapport with the customer. Remember, it's customers who rate your performance, not photocopying machines.'

'Ah, so you think I should chat up the customer a bit more? If I'd done that I thought you'd criticise me for timewasting.'

'No, remember when you are out on calls you are the interface with the customer. As far as they are concerned, you *are* Xerox. I'm confident that if you invested some time talking with the customer it would improve your feedback ratings. Give it a go.'

On his next call, to a big legal firm near the Barbican, Mark, ever willing to learn, experimented with a bit more chitchat.

'What a beautiful setup you have here,' Mark said, as a secretary guided him along plush corridors, the walls displaying colourful works of original art. 'I bet the legal fees you charge are quite something to pay for all this.'

They had reached the faulty photocopier and Mark put his rucksack down beside it.

'I can assure you that our clients value our services and find our fees competitive,' the secretary replied indignantly.

'Sorry, I didn't mean to suggest you were ripping them off.' Mark decided to change tack. 'Fancy being so close to the Barbican. Do you get to see any of the shows?'

'No,' said the secretary rather curtly. 'I have a long commute home and we are often kept working late.'

Oh, what a pity, I'm sorry to hear that. Where's home?'

'Hanwell, but what's it to you?'

'Oh, sorry, I didn't mean to seem nosey. Well, what seems to be the problem with the copier?'

'That's for you to decide,' she said, sounding decidedly shirty. 'The paper keeps jamming. We've cleared it a few times but it just happens again and cuts out.'

'Hmm, I expect someone's been careless restocking the tray. Not over-loading it and getting the paper straight is vital.'

'That's as maybe.'

'Right, well leave me to it and I'll get it sorted. Where shall I find you when I'm done?'

'Back along the corridor. I'm in the room on the right before you reach the lifts.'

She left and Mark opened up the machine, swiftly diagnosed the cause of the paper jams, made the necessary adjustments and double-checked that the machine was working properly.

'All done,' he said having retraced his steps along the corridor, pausing occasionally to admire a painting.

'Thanks,' she said, not looking up. 'Can you find your own way out?'

'Sure,' said Mark. 'Don't hesitate to call us if there's a problem. That's what we're here for. Have a nice day.'

Outside the sun was shining and Mark and Bert sat on a bench beside a raised flower bed full of colourful tulips.

'Well,' said Bert, 'how do you think that went?'

'I don't think we hit it off. She seemed a bit pissed off really.'

'Yep, wrong sort of conversation. Let's see if she's provided any feedback.' Bert looked at his smart phone. 'As I feared, one star. And she's added a comment: "Wasted time chatting."'

'But I thought you wanted me to engage with the customer, not just busy myself fixing the machine.'

'I do, but I obviously didn't make myself clear. The customer needs to find the conversation relevant to the job in hand, not stuff about where they live and certainly not anything they might see as criticisms of them or their business.'

'Bloody hell, there's more to this than I thought.'

'Tell you what, try this. Minimise any conversation until you reach the copier. Immediately open it up and then ask the customer some questions about the problem they've experienced. Avoid blaming anyone or anything and, when you've finished asking questions, get your tools out and set to work.'

The next visit was to the Bank of England. They had to wait in reception, an area remarkably like a side-chapel in a cathedral, while a man in a top hat and a pink jacket phoned the relevant department. After a short while a young man appeared and escorted them to the inner sanctum.

'My name is Thomas. Have you been here before?' the young man asked.

'No,' Mark replied. 'I'm Mark, pleased to meet you. From the outside, you'd never guess there was a garden inside here.'

'Yes, unfortunately the Governor's offices overlook it so we are not allowed access.'

They went up in a lift and Thomas guided them to the photocopier. Mark put down his rucksack and opened up the machine. He turned to Thomas.

'What seems to be the problem?'

'As you can see the warning light keeps flashing. We've tried all the usual stuff but it refuses to cooperate.'

'Has the paper been jamming?'

'No, we checked for that.'

'Have you tried switching it off and then on again?

'Yes, but the warning light came back on.'

'Hmm, that's a bit of a puzzle,' said Mark. 'But we're here to solve it. Anything else you can tell me?'

'No, sorry not to be more helpful.' Then he added as an afterthought, 'The decorators were in here over the weekend. I guess they had to move the machine, might that have mucked things up?'

'Could be,' said Mark, 'I thought I could smell fresh paint. Anyway, thanks for your help. Leave it to me. I'll see what I can do.'

'Good luck,' said Thomas. 'Call this number when you're done and I'll come and escort you out.'

Thomas left and Mark got to work, systematically working through the diagnostic process while Bert watched. The problem was quite complex but after half an hour the photocopier was running normally. Thomas returned and Mark gave him a demonstration.

'Great! I won't ask you what was wrong with it. Probably be over my head.'

'I'll not bore you with the details. Suffice to say it should be OK now but don't hesitate to call again if there are more problems.'

Outside, sitting on a bench whilst admiring the west façade of the Royal Exchange, Bert said, 'How did you feel that went?'

'Pretty well, I guess. Let's wait to see how he rated the visit.'

Bert looked at his smart phone. 'Nothing there yet, but I'm sure that young man will have been impressed. A business-like conversation and the problem fixed, what more could you ask for?'

The feedback came in: 5 stars, excellent.

'Wow, at last!' said Mark. 'Thanks so much for all your help. I think I've got it now.'

Bert, stood up and shook Mark's hand. 'Well done, young man. You're a quick learner. You'll go far.'

After a couple of years, with consistently good ratings, Mark moved on and took a better paid job with Siemens, doing call-outs to customers' homes, servicing washing machines and dishwashers. Mark stuck to his winning formula: minimise chitchat, open up the machine, ask the customer some diagnostic questions, get to work and fix the problem. Job done. But after his first week, the feedback he was getting left him in no doubt that something was wrong. Very wrong.

He arranged to meet up with Bert, his old mentor at Xerox. They met in a pub.

'So, what's the problem?' asked Bert. 'Had second thoughts about leaving? I told you you'd regret it.'

'At this rate I'll get the sack and be begging to come back,' said Mark gloomily. 'Trouble is I'm getting low ratings and crap customer feedback and I can't work out why.'

'Give me some examples.'

Mark pushed a piece of paper over the table. 'Doesn't make for happy reading I'm afraid.'

Bert picked up the A4 sheet and read:

A ditherer. Send someone who knows what they're doing next time.

Lacking in confidence. Pulled the machine out, took the lid off and then expected me to tell him what was wrong with it.

Seemed unsure of himself. Kept asking me questions when he should have been fixing the problem.

I wanted him to fix the machine. He seemed to want me to fix it!

He could see I wanted to collect the kids from school, but he just kept pestering me with silly questions.

Didn't inspire confidence. Seemed unsure what to do.

'Hmm,' said Bert, 'I see what you mean.'

'What do you think I'm doing wrong?'

'Well,' Bert shook his head, 'seems like you've forgotten what I taught you.'

'Oh, come on, I'm doing exactly what you taught me and it isn't working.'

'No, you're making the biggest mistake of all. You're just repeating what worked on calls to business premises. Now you're going into people's homes: different clientele, different environment, needs a different approach.'

'So, it's back to the drawing board then?'

'Yep,' said Bert, 'you got complacent and didn't realise you were on a new learning curve. Life's one learning curve after another.'

The Litter Patrol

A litter picking stick was one of many things Daphne's husband left behind when he suddenly died from an aneurysm. It nestled unobtrusively amongst a variety of walking sticks in an umbrella stand in the hall.

For many years, her husband had ventured out every Sunday morning collecting litter. He was a nonbeliever who nonetheless maintained that Sundays should be set aside for good works. Far from Sundays being a day of rest, in addition to picking up litter in the mornings, the afternoons were devoted to visiting or phoning friends who were unwell and writing newsy emails to a couple of pen friends. On Sundays he also took sole charge of producing the evening meal and clearing up afterwards.

In the weeks immediately after her husband's unexpected death, Daphne came to dread Sundays. She found it easy to busy herself on weekdays: meeting friends, participating in various u3a groups, going to her Tai Chi classes for the over-seventies. She knew she ought to set to work sorting out her husband's possessions but every Sunday she tended to feel lethargic and succumbed to melancholy. She knew this was foolish and that she should pull herself together.

One Sunday morning, an empty day stretching ahead of her, Daphne was sitting thinking about her dear, departed husband when the doorbell rang. She opened the front door to find a young lad standing in the porch. She guessed he was about sixteen or seventeen. He looked vaguely familiar and she tried to place him. Had he been at her husband's funeral? It had been well attended and she wasn't sure.

'Forgive me for disturbing you, Mrs Blencowe,' the young man said. 'You probably don't know me, I'm Georgie, Georgie Ashworth,' he paused and ran a hand through a generous mop of blonde hair. 'I knew your husband and often saw him on his litter round.'

'Oh, really. That's nice.'

'I'm so sorry for your loss. Yes, we often had good chats. Your husband was an inspiration.'

'Thank you, that's very touching. I know he enjoyed chatting to people. I sometimes wondered if picking up litter was just his excuse to get out of the house.'

The young man smiled. 'Anyway, I was wondering if I could borrow his litter picker. I'd very much like to take over where he left off....... so to speak.'

Without a moment's hesitation Daphne said, 'That's very thoughtful of you but I'm planning to start doing the litter patrol myself.'

'Oh, I see,' said Georgie, clearly taken aback. 'Well of course, if you're quite sure it won't be too much for you. I'm more than happy to take it on.'

'No, I'll do it,' Daphne replied firmly. 'My husband always

sang the praises of his litter stick. He often joked that whoever invented it deserved a knighthood.'

'Well, if you're quite sure,' said Georgie, sounding disappointed, perhaps even a little resentful. 'Please let me know if you change your mind. It would be an honour to follow in your husband's footsteps.'

And with that he left, carefully closing the front gate behind him and giving Daphne a quick wave as he disappeared behind the yew hedge. Daphne retreated to the kitchen and made herself a cup of coffee. Her spontaneous decision to do the litter on Sunday mornings had taken her by surprise. She'd been panicked by the thought of handing over her husband's litter picker to a complete stranger. Things were still too raw. She simply wasn't ready to start disposing of her husband's many possessions.

She finished her coffee and visited the umbrella stand. There, exactly where her husband had left it, was the litter picking stick. A little gingerly, she picked it up and squeezed the lever on the handle, the jaws closed and opened again as soon as she released it. She was reminded of a wooden toy her children used to play with when they were small: a crocodile painted bright green with jaws that opened and closed as it was pulled along.

She decided to give the litter stick a practice run and scattered some pieces of paper over the kitchen floor. She found that gathering them up and depositing them in a bin was straightforward, and all achieved without having to bend: a great relief since she had arthritic joints and often suffered lower back pain.

Next Sunday Daphne rose early, feeling determined and purposeful. After having a poached egg on toast for breakfast, she donned her coat and gardening gloves, and, clutching the stick and a plastic bag, ventured out. She felt absurdly adventurous.

She followed the route she believed her husband used to take, basically a triangle of residential roads, including a small park with a children's play area tucked away in one corner. The only shop was a small Tesco's that had recently opened in what had been a Victorian pub. Daphne found very little litter on the pavements outside residential houses but the park and the area immediately outside the Tesco store kept her busy: cigarette ends, sweet wrappers, empty drink cans, discarded tissues, plastic water bottles, shop receipts and sandwich packets. The litter picker coped with it all.

Daphne was delighted to find that all the people she met greeted her warmly - mums and dads watching their children playing in the park, a delivery driver clambering out of his cab outside Tesco's, a man clipping his privet hedge, a woman sweeping her front path.

When Daphne got back home she felt good, very good. She smiled at the litter stick as she returned it to its place in the umbrella stand, and sat down to recover from her exertions. Litter picking had been surprisingly enjoyable, even invigorating. No wonder her husband had gone out every Sunday morning and always returned sounding so upbeat.

Her son, a solicitor living in Manchester, telephoned and Daphne told him about her adventures.

'That's great, Mum, but be sure not to overdue it.'

'It's surprisingly easy. It only takes an hour or so and the people I meet are so appreciative.'

'Gosh, you must be cutting corners. I remember it used to take Dad at least three hours.'

'I can't imagine how it could have taken him so long. I didn't exactly hurry and I even had time to stop and talk to some people. Quite a doddle. Anyway, there's help if I need it. A young man has already called and asked if he can take over. He wanted to use your father's litter stick and seemed disappointed when I said I'd do it.'

'Did he say who he was?'

'His name was Georgie something - I've forgotten the surname. He seemed to be something of a fan, but I don't recall your father ever mentioning him.'

The next Sunday, it was early November and starting to get cold, there was a brisk wind and trapping fluttering bits of paper with the picker was proving troublesome. A helpful man put his foot on a discarded newspaper just as it threatened to become airborne.

'Thank you,' Daphne beamed, successfully trapping the newspaper with her stick.

'Only too glad to be of assistance.' The man smiled and touched the peak of his baseball cap. 'It's so good to see someone doing their bit for the local community.'

'I'm following in my late husband's footsteps. Every Sunday for many years he ventured out picking up litter in this area.'

The man nodded. 'Yes, I know. I knew your husband quite well. He often stopped for a chat, him and his young helper. They made a fine pair.'

'He had a helper?' Daphne asked.

'Oh, yes. More often than not he was accompanied by a young lad, a striking young fellow with lots of blonde hair……. Georgie, that was his name. They seemed close. Naturally I assumed he was your son.'

Daphne returned home and put the litter stick back in the umbrella stand. Thank goodness, she thought, those jaws can't talk.

The Novice

Up until now, I've been the only person in the world to know that I cheated, not once but twice. Quite a thought that: approximately seven billion people on the planet and I'm the only one to know my guilty secret. It's almost a shame to spoil it by coming clean about what happened. But what the hell, it was a few years ago and no one got hurt. Well, I say 'no one' but who does that include? Are animals no ones?

Where to start?

At the time, more or less on a whim, I'd bought my uncle's farm. He wanted to retire and I, just turned forty, had made a packet from selling my recruitment agency. We had a number of lucrative contracts hiring overseas workers for the NHS, but the press were increasingly hostile. Too much hassle, I wanted out. So, virtually overnight, I became a multi-millionaire and the owner of a 500 acre farm with a limestone farmhouse, numerous rundown barns and outhouses, five farm workers and an award winning herd of 100 Jersey cattle, with doleful eyes and long eyelashes.

I've always had a soft spot for animals. When I was a kid we had cats and dogs, rabbits and gerbils too. I can still remember all their names and the elaborate burial ceremonies in the garden when they died. My sister was crazy about horses so we had a pony too. All quite innocent and soppy so you'll understand that suddenly owning a commercial farm raised the bar considerably. But, being a conscientious sort of bloke and, if I'm honest, not wanting to make a fool of myself (oh, the naivety!), I enrolled on a City & Guilds course run by the local Agricultural College.

I was, of course, a complete misfit: middle-aged, wealthy and over-confident. By contrast, my fellow students, all young apprentices on day-release from farms in the College's catchment area, were spotty, penniless and bolshie. We attended lectures in the mornings - bad ones, disorganized and boring - and donned wellies and undertook practicals in the afternoons. Predictably, the apprentices struggled in the mornings while I excelled and our roles were dramatically reversed in the afternoons, when they were in their element and I was a ham-fisted novice.

At various stages throughout the course we had to take proficiency tests. External examiners would appear, looking suitably stern, dressed incongruously in white overalls, clutching clip-boards.

The first proficiency test was disbudding - removing the horn buds on six-week old calves using a hot-iron. The need to do this was, for me, a revelation. I had never given a moment's thought to cows' horns and the damage they could inflict if they were allowed to grow. For the apprentices, however, not only was the need to disbud common knowledge, but they were already well practised in the procedure. For them it was a doddle.

We'd had a few practice runs before the day of the test and I, cocky bugger, was sure I'd got the hang of it. First, catch the calf and restrain it. Second, run your thumb along the channel that runs diagonally from the calf's eye to its ear. Third, locate the junction about half way between the two. Fourth, keep your thumb on the spot and, using a syringe, inject the anaesthetic. Fifth, do the same on the other side. Sixth, wait five minutes. Seventh, stick a pin into each bud to check the anaesthetic has taken effect. Eighth, if the calf doesn't flinch, burn off each bud. Job done. Easy-peasy.

In the light of what I'm about to confess, I should perhaps quote a relevant passage from the handout we'd been given: *The whole process to remove both buds should take no longer than 10 minutes and the calf should not struggle at any stage during the procedure. A stressed calf means a stressed worker, which is self-perpetuating. The use of a local anaesthetic is a legal requirement when hot-iron disbudding.*

The day came for us to take the proficiency test with an unsmiling external examiner in attendance. As I waited for the opportunity to demonstrate my newfound prowess, I was surprised to find myself feeling apprehensive. This was of course absurd since passing the test didn't really matter to me and throughout my previous life I'd always taken exams in my stride. When my turn came, feigning calm competence, I restrained a hapless calf, used my thumb to locate the correct place for the anaesthetic, inserted the needle and squeezed the plunger on the syringe.

I'd administered about half the dose when I realised I'd

inserted the needle into the end of my own thumb! Fortunately the examiner was busy noting something on his clipboard so I surreptitiously withdrew the needle, moved my thumb aside and put what remained of the anaesthetic into the calf. Meanwhile, my thumb went numb and a strange fizziness spread rapidly up my left arm. I remember wondering if the anaesthetic might reach my heart but, not wanting to do anything that might jeopardise my first proficiency test, I remained stoical. I refilled the syringe and injected aesthetic into the other side of the calf's head without mishap. When I stuck the pin into the left horn, the poor calf jumped. The examiner looked puzzled but told me to carry on regardless.

Quite undeservedly, I passed the test and wasn't asked to explain why my calf was the only one to put up such a heroic struggle. It took the rest of the day for the effects of the anaesthetic to wear off and for my arm to feel normal.

Castration brought about my second misadventure. Our lecturer had demonstrated the procedure and I'll spare you the gory details, but suffice to say that testicles are slippery things with a strong sense of self-preservation. Once exposed by cutting through the scrotum, they quickly take fright and ascend, like a high speed elevator, into the body cavity. Once there, tantalisingly just out of reach, they stubbornly refuse to come back down. Our lecturer had warned us about this and emphasized the importance of blocking the escape route by using your fingers in a swift scissor movement.

When I first attempted castration, we happened to be visiting a farm where the farmer, quite understandably, was worried we might make a hash of things. He insisted that all the testicles, once removed, should be placed in a large kidney dish. At intervals throughout the afternoon, the farmer would suddenly appear and check that the dish contained an even number of testicles.

Fortunately, when it was my turn to wield the knife, the farmer wasn't in attendance. Neither was our lecturer who, I think, had gone behind a wall for a quick pee. Undaunted, I cut open the scrotum and grabbed one slippery testicle but failed to catch the other one. To my horror, it made a rapid ascent and stopped, quivering, within sight but just out of reach. Fearing the farmer's imminent return, I made a quick decision: I severed one testicle, stuffed it into my pocket and released the calf with the other testicle still intact.

The lecturer returned, doing up his zip, and was surprised to find how swiftly I'd completed the procedure. When the farmer next appeared to do a spot-check, he found an even number of testicles in the kidney dish. Fortunately, it didn't seem to occur to him to count the calves in the 'done' pen, multiply by two and see if the answer tallied with the testicles in the dish.

Later, cruising along the motorway in my Bentley, I tossed my guilty secret out of the window onto the central reservation. In my rear view mirror, I watched a red kite swoop down and carry the unexpected delicacy away.

The Guide

Basil had no idea that anyone had complained. As far as he was aware, his customers had always been enthralled, gathering round to catch his every word above the background noise of passing traffic, laughing appreciatively at his well-rehearsed jokes. But a curt email conveyed the bad news: someone had accused him of making insensitive and offensive remarks. Insensitive *and* offensive - not just one, but both.

Appalled, Basil read the email again. Apparently, an unidentified person or persons had reported him to the Institute of Tourist Guiding, his professional body, and he was summoned to a formal hearing to explain himself.

His hard-earned Blue Badge was clearly in jeopardy.

Basil cast his mind back over the tours he had led around the monuments in Trafalgar Square: two kings, two generals and one admiral: all white, all men. The email from the Institute gave no indication of how far back he should go. He assumed the complaint must have been fairly recent. He usually conducted four tours a week, two on Wednesdays and two on Fridays. How could he possibly work out which group had harboured the anonymous complainant?

Not surprisingly, his memory of the participants was hazy. Invariably they were a sea of nondescript faces: fifteen or so people obediently following him as he led them around the Square, clustering round each monument as they listened to his spiel. He knew he should distribute his eye contact in more or less equal measure to avoid becoming fixated on anyone in particular. However, try as he might, he found it difficult to remain impartial. He couldn't help having favourites: people who appeared to hang on his every word, people who nodded and smiled, people who asked sensible questions (especially those he could answer), young, attractive females he secretly fancied. Oh lord, might one of those have thought he was leering at them?

How could he possibly know who he had offended?

Basil had always found it difficult to judge the extent to which foreign visitors on his tours were content with his performance. They were more difficult to fathom. Perhaps he'd offended someone in the Japanese group that he'd led round the Square recently? Might they have sensed his irritation with their ceaseless giggling and their reluctance to ask any questions? Had they thought him disrespectful when he failed to return their bows at the end of the tour?

Or might he have upset the Indians in one of his groups when he'd described how, in 1857 at the ripe old age of 62 (Basil's age), Major General Sir Henry Havelock had helped to put down the Indian Mutiny. Perhaps they objected to his enthusiastic description of how Havelock had led the final charge that resulted in the deaths of thousands of rebels. Had he sounded a touch too jingoistic? Or maybe it had been when, standing at the other plinth and gazing up at the magnificent bronze of Major General Sir Charles Napier, he had related how the general had conquered Sind in 1843, using cannon fire to slaughter huge numbers of Sindi and Baluchi soldiers. Could that have upset someone? And what about dear Nelson standing victoriously on the top of his column? Might some French tourists have taken offence when he waxed lyrical about the Admiral's victories over Napoleon?

The possibilities were endless.

Maybe he'd upset a fat person - there had always been plenty of those in his groups - with his mickey-taking about George IV's considerable girth. He always told the story of how Chantry, the creator of the bronze, had used artistic licence to slim the king down and, having done so, still put him astride a horse with all four legs firmly planted on the ground - a first in equestrian bronzes. Yes, thinking back, Basil could see how people who were overweight might have objected to the way he cheerfully recounted how the king had died a morbidly obese drunkard. Still, facts are facts. Why should he be economical with the truth just because some people in his group stuffed their faces with junk food?

Basil became increasingly indignant as he realised the possibilities of inadvertently causing offence were endless. Yet, he reminded himself, he'd been guiding folk around Trafalgar Square for ten years without mishap. Was it possible that he'd become too complacent, a little too sure of himself? Basil quickly pushed the thought aside. He mustn't succumb to self-doubt in his hour of need.

Maybe someone had objected to the way he always poo-pooed recent demands to remove the bronzes of the two

Victorian generals, to drag them from their pedestals and fling them in the Thames. He always joked that they'd probably be replaced with someone considered more worthy: someone black or transgender. As far as he could judge, his audiences had always shared his utter disdain for anything "woke".

Might the problem have resulted from something he'd said about the magnificent statue of Charles I astride his horse - the oldest bronze in London. Surely not. As far as he was aware, people had always enjoyed listening to him relating the story of how Cromwell's lot had been hoodwinked by a brazier called John Rivet. How, during the Civil War, the Puritans had ordered him to destroy the statue but instead he'd buried the whole thing - no mean feat as it was over 9ft tall and 8ft long - and pretended he'd broken it up by selling trinkets supposedly made from the metal. Then, after the Restoration, how Rivet had dug up the statue and sold it at a vast profit to Charles II who'd had it erected where it stands today, gazing down Whitehall at the site where his martyred father had been beheaded. He always relished telling the story of Rivet's blatant opportunism. How could anyone possibly object? Puritans he supposed.

Ah well, Basil reflected, it was obviously easy to upset people without even knowing he was doing so.

Perhaps it was nothing to do with his well-rehearsed storytelling. Maybe he'd caused offence with an off-the-cuff comment, one of his many spontaneous ad libs. Perhaps it was that woman with mobility problems who'd had trouble keeping up with the group. Had he been short with her when she kept asking him to repeat what she'd missed? Or perhaps it was someone in the group who'd sympathised with that annoying woman carrying a placard saying 'Be Kind to Pigeons'. She had moved amongst his group encouraging them to feed the pigeons and distributing little packets of bird food. He'd tried to ignore her but eventually he'd lost his patience, telling her in no uncertain terms that he thought the pigeons were a damned nuisance - always crapping on the statues. Maybe someone in his group, possibly a pigeon-lover, had thought him unduly harsh.

Might he have fallen foul of an undercover inspector, he wondered. He knew he'd been checked out a couple of times before because, once the tourists had dispersed, the inspectors had done the decent thing and made themselves known to him. But they'd both been men of more or less his own age, seemingly full of admiration for his smooth patter. They had been amused by Basil's Union Jack tie but gently recommended that he discontinued wearing his UKIP lapel badge.

Then Basil had a dreadful thought. Might he have upset a female inspector who sneakily hadn't declared herself? Someone younger than him: perhaps a feminist, maybe even a lesbian!

It was hopeless. Basil was at a total loss. However, though not given to self-reflection, the more he thought about it, the more he could see how some people might find him too outspoken, perhaps even too opinionated.

Then the truth dawned on him. The complaint must be something to do with the disparaging remarks he always made about the Fourth Plinth. He left people in no doubt that he disapproved of the use of the plinth for temporary displays of contemporary art. He had always made it clear that modern art was definitely not his thing. Someone must have objected to him ridiculing the most recent display: a dollop of whipped cream with an assortment of toppings, including a cherry, a fly and a drone. He proudly told his groups how, back in 2009, he'd volunteered to be one of the 2,400 people who spent an hour on the plinth. Sadly, he hadn't been selected but, he told his audiences, if he had been he was going to spend his time on the plinth displaying a huge placard saying 'Maggie Thatcher should be standing here'.

Basil decided to take the only honourable course open to him: he wrote to the Institute declining to attend the hearing and tending his resignation forthwith. He reckoned it was better to be a Fourth Plinth martyr than to be forced to toe the official line. Far better to jump before suffering the indignity of being pushed.

He was not for turning! He felt sure that Maggie Thatcher, were she still alive, would approve.

A few days later Basil received a reply from the Institute. They thanked him for his distinguished service as a Blue Guide and accepted his resignation with regret. They went on to say that, had he chosen to attend the hearing, they were sure the matter could have been resolved amicably.

'Resolved amicably'? Perhaps he'd been hasty in tending his resignation. Maybe his remarks about the absurdity of the Fourth Plinth had not, after all, been the problem.

He *had* to know.

He phoned the Institute and was amazed to learn that the complaint had been lodged by a great-great grandson of Major General Sir Charles Napier. Apparently, he had written to the Institute complaining that Basil had been disrespectful about his distinguished relative.

Basil's heart sank. How absurd that anyone, even a distant

relative of the General, could object to him passing round a laminated cartoon of Napier receiving homage from 3,000 Sindi chieftains. In stark contrast to the formality of his statue, the eyewitness sketch showed what the General had actually looked like, with a huge, beaked nose and a beard that fell in wild profusion to his chest. He was dressed inappropriately in an old flannel jacket, dirty white trousers and a peaked hunting cap. Basil relished telling his captive audiences that it was no wonder the General's soldiers had always referred to him as 'Old Fagin'.

Basil reflected ruefully that an anonymous sketch drawn in 1844, not his outspoken views on, well, just about everything, had been the cause of his downfall.

The Bastard

Ian was happy - blissfully happy. At the age of only 42 he'd landed his dream job. He'd been recruited by head-hunters on behalf of an organisation that had grown rapidly through a series of ill-advised acquisitions and mergers. Ian's brief, as the newly appointed chief executive, was to sort out the mess and return the organisation to profitability. The board was impatient for results and so was Ian, who stood to gain a handsome performance-related bonus.

At his interview, the board members of the parent company had been impressed by Ian's vigour and seemingly invincible self-confidence.

'I'm not interested in problems,' he'd announced, pausing momentarily to make eye-contact with each member of the panel in turn, 'I'm interested in solutions!'

'Perhaps you could elucidate. Surely problems are the precursors to solutions?' the chairman had asked, looking puzzled. 'You can't have one without the other.'

Ian smiled, like a teacher straining to be patient with a slow-witted child. 'Don't misunderstand me. I'm not saying problems aren't important, of course they are. But I prefer to think of them as challenges - challenges in search of solutions. Problems are depressing, challenges are exciting! It's too easy to get bogged down with problems.'

'I see,' said the chairman, not at all sure that he did. 'Well, whatever you call them, problems or challenges, we've got plenty of them.'

'Trust me,' beamed Ian, 'I'll get it sorted.'

And they had.

Once in post, Ian set to work with his usual vigour: working long hours, forever on the move, jiggling his legs, striding around clicking his fingers, straightening pictures, running his fingers through his hair, dropping in on people unexpectedly. His first action was to assemble his hapless team and give them a pep talk, the gist of which had been, 'Don't bother me with problems. Only come to me with solutions.'

But Ian's team found it difficult to adjust to this new approach, convinced that problems not only existed, but that many of the ones they were wrestling with were insoluble. It didn't help that Ian's predecessor had *loved* having problems to ponder, even listing them on a white board in his office, with curtains that could be discreetly drawn to shield them from visitors. It was entirely understandable, therefore, that they often lapsed, but whenever they mentioned the P-word, Ian would explode. 'Solutions,' he'd yell, 'I want SOLUTIONS!'

It didn't take long for a solution - though not the sort Ian had in mind - to dawn on Ian's top team: to keep their heads down, minimise any contact with Ian and never, ever, admit to having any problems.

Inevitably, Ian became increasingly frustrated with the lack of progress. The board too, were starting to wonder whether they'd appointed the right man. When, they asked, would he start to deliver the results they'd entrusted him to deliver? After one particularly uncomfortable board meeting, during which Ian could only bluster, he gathered his team together once more to emphasise the importance of finding solutions. 'That's what you're paid for - to identify CHALLENGES and produce fucking SOLUTIONS!'

But it was to no avail. The more Ian ranted, the more his direct reports covered up their problems and increasingly suffered from solution paralysis.

One evening, after a particularly exasperating day when, once again, he'd confronted his top team, demanding to know why they were being secretive, only to be greeted with sheepish looks, he complained to his girlfriend, Cherise. 'They're a bunch of wankers. I think they're deliberately avoiding me, ganging up on me.'

'I'm not surprised,' said Cherise, scantily clad and gazing into a mirror whilst plucking her eyebrows. 'They'll have worked out what a shit you are by now.'

'That's enough of your cheek,' grumbled Ian. 'Let's go to bed.'

'Just coming, dad.'

Ian had a fast turnaround in girlfriends, tiring of them quickly and moving on. Cherise, his latest, was twenty years younger than him. He was irritated when she called him dad but he was prepared to grin and bear it because of the amazing sex. She was a gymnast, capable of performing extraordinary contortions, and seemingly never tiring of Ian's vigorous love-making.

One day Ian went to a seminar at the Institute of Directors. It was rare for him to subject himself to talk-shops. He found it an ordeal to sit still and listen for protracted periods. He planned to cut his losses, skip the afternoon session and leave after lunch. However, the last speaker of the morning, an American consultant he had vaguely heard of, captured his attention. He spoke persuasively about the benefits of staff attitude surveys, in particular a process he called 360-degree feedback. Ian was immediately attracted to the idea. It promised to be the solution he craved: a way to confront his team with further evidence of their incompetence, perhaps even to provide him with data he could use to dismiss them.

The next day Ian contacted the speaker, a Dr Tom Abott, and hired him to conduct a 360-degree survey.

A contract duly arrived from Dr Abott's American headquarters, and Ian signed off the eyewatering daily fee. After a few weeks, a team of consultants got to work using a questionnaire that invited staff to give detailed, anonymous feedback about their managers. Ian's staff, not used to being consulted or listened to, relished the opportunity to have their say. Accordingly, the response rate was over 90 per cent – the highest ever in Tom's vast experience of conducting surveys of this kind.

The questionnaires were duly analysed and Tom arranged to meet Ian to give him a preliminary overview of the findings prior to them being shared with the management group. They met over dinner at Tom's lavish London club. After some inconsequential chat, Ian said, 'Come on man, let's cut to the chase. What does the feedback show?'

Tom smiled, 'Are you quite sure you want to know?'

'Come on, give it to me straight. What does it say about my top team?'

'It's not good, not good at all.'

'Not a surprise. Come on man, stop farting about.'

Tom called a nearby waiter over. 'Please get this man another drink.' Then he turned to Ian. 'Remind me, why did you think conducting a staff survey was a good idea? Specifically, what did you hope to gain?'

'I told you before. I'm expecting it to confirm my view that my top team are a bunch of incompetent wankers.'

'Well, I think you'll be disappointed. The overwhelming finding is that you're impossible to work with. Specifically, that you're unhelpful, unapproachable and a foul-mouthed bastard.'

'The fuckers! I might have guessed, they're just using the survey to get back at me. I should never have agreed to it being anonymous.'

Tom, well versed in dealing with senior managers in a state of denial when confronted with their feedback, reassured Ian. 'If you want to change their perceptions, you'll have to change your behaviour. I can help you with that.'

The plan was simple. For one year, Ian would spend two hours every working day talking with staff, listening to their problems and helping them to think through solutions. When the year was up, the survey would be repeated to measure the extent of progress.

Cherise giggled when Ian told her about the plan. They were in bed, temporarily exhausted after another bout of love-making. 'Go on, pull the other one, you'll never manage that. A leopard can't change its spots.'

Ian, becoming increasingly tired of Cherise and her tendency to trot out clichés, snapped back, 'Fuck off, it'll happen, you'll see.' He smiled to himself, knowing it was unlikely she'd still be around in a year's time.

Ian made a superhuman effort and for a year, coached by Tom, he suppressed his old ways and stuck to the plan. He no longer swore and he actively encouraged people to seek his help in finding solutions to problems, even allowing them to use the P-word. He became skilled at helping people to explore the pros and cons of different courses of action, gently steering them towards the best option, and supporting them as they implemented whatever had been agreed. He was genuinely surprised by the quality of the ideas that were forthcoming, many of them resulting in significant improvements and cost-saving efficiencies.

All in all, Ian felt very pleased with himself and the board, welcoming the results, formally minuted their congratulations.

The year passed quickly. Cherise had been replaced by Cheril, only ten years younger than him (he was no longer called dad) and regrettably not as agile as Cherise, but better educated (fewer clichés). The time had come to repeat the survey. Once again, the response rate was high and, as before, Tom and Ian met in the lavish comfort of Tom's club to discuss the results. By now, having worked closely together for a year, the two men knew each other well.

'So, come on, Tom, spit it out. What does the survey show?'

'As expected, definite progress.' Tom smiled. 'Your efforts have paid off. I'm happy to report that your staff now think you're a *cunning* bastard!'

The Impossible Objects Company

Once upon a time an entrepreneur called Dr Do had a brilliant idea. His ideas usually came to him when wallowing in a hot bath, but this one happened in a meeting with his financial adviser. Dr Do was a wealthy man, having made a fortune inventing acronyms, idioms and mnemonics. Dr Do (first name Can) hated meetings. He found them boring and he resented the way they gobbled up time when he could be busy 'doing'. It didn't help that his financial adviser was also boring, tending to drone on about tax avoidance and offshore bonds.

Dr Do, when bored by boring meetings with boring people, passed the time by doodling. But, being an entrepreneur, his doodles had the potential to turn into something useful, so he specialised in doodling geometric shapes with metaphorical names such as U-shapes, T-shapes, hourglass-shapes, bell-shapes, dog-bone shapes, bowtie-shapes, Z-shapes (which turned sideways miraculously became N-shapes) and so on.

As his financial adviser droned on about doubtful, but apparently legal, ways to avoid inheritance tax, Dr Do doodled a

U-shape lying on its side and, after adding shading, it became a shape like this:

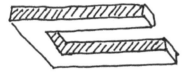

Then he drew it again like this:

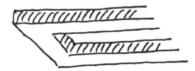

Then he joined up the six open ends and it suddenly became this:

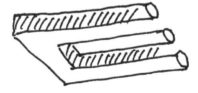

Dr Do became enormously excited, as he was prone to do, realising that he'd stumbled upon an impossible object. He interrupted his financial adviser in mid-flow, to announce that he was going to patent his impossible object, form *The Impossible Objects Company*, and corner the market in impossible objects.

Being a doer, Dr Do, whilst waiting impatiently in the Patents Office, turned his customary doodle of a triangle into this:

Within a few months, having conjured up more impossible objects, Dr Do, even though he was a great doer, simply couldn't keep pace with the demand he'd created for impossible objects. So, with great reluctance, he recruited three helpers: Mr Review, Mr Conclude, and Mr Plan. Dr Do hoped that their diverse skills would dovetail (he was actively experimenting with dovetail doodles) to produce synergy, where their different skills would combine to produce more than the sum of their individual parts.

However, now that there were four of them, and surprisingly for such a brilliant man this was an implication Dr Do had failed to foresee, they needed to have meetings. Despite the fact that Dr Do had created his first impossible object in a meeting, he hated the way they tended to drone on and on, bogged down with minutiae. The only exceptions, and he couldn't bring himself to think of them as meetings, were brainstorming sessions, where he bounced ideas off other doers in an exhilarating surge of creativity.

Dr Do was, therefore, alarmed to find that meetings between the four of them were bereft of ideas, not creative, not fun and dragged on for far too long. This was because Mr Review was ultra cautious and always wanted to examine everything very thoroughly. If you showed him a prototype of an impossible object, as Dr Do did frequently, Mr Review would examine it from all possible angles and, even when he'd done so, would remain non-committal, wanting more time to 'mull it over' and 'sleep on it' before committing himself.

Meetings between them also lacked lustre because Mr Conclude liked everything to be logical, neat and tidy. He couldn't stand loose ends. Impossible objects were, therefore, intensely irritating to Mr Conclude. For him anything impossible was imperfect. When Dr Do showed him the prototype of an impossible object, he'd devote all his energies to trying to make it possible. Dr Do considered this nothing short of sacrilegious - maintaining, not unreasonably, that the whole point of an impossible object was that it was impossible. The more impossible, the better.

Meetings between them also went badly because Mr Plan liked everything to be practical and organised. He didn't like surprises, preferring everything to be prescribed, to follow a preordained route. He'd therefore become agitated with Dr Do's ill-disciplined bursts of spontaneity. When Dr Do showed him the prototype of an impossible object, he'd instantly start planning uses for it. In Dr Do's view this was a futile exercise since impossible objects were supposed to be useless. The more useless, the better.

So, with these differing inclinations, you can imagine that meetings between the four men became progressively impossible. So much so, that Dr Do toyed with the idea of expanding *The Impossible Objects Company* to include a division that specialised in impossible meetings.

One day, seated at the round-table where they held their impossible meetings, they were, as usual, all diversely busy: Dr Do was doodling, trying to square a circle; Mr Review was busy conducting a painstaking review of the latest impossible object; Mr Conclude was busy trying to make it possible; and Mr Plan was busy planning uses for it. Dr Do, simultaneously exasperated by the lack of progress and intrigued that yet again they were going round in circles, drew this:

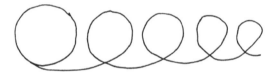

He fiddled with it for a while, turning it into an oval, into an ellipse, into a wheel (ugh, much too useful!) when, aimlessly as was his wont, he drew a fresh circle and doodled their names onto it to reflect their seating positions. It looked like this:

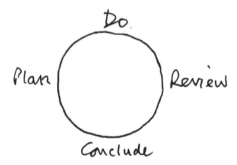

Gazing at the seating plan he'd drawn, Dr Do had one of his lightbulb moments. Suddenly he understood that, despite intellectually subscribing to the idea of synergetic working, he was guilty of wanting his three colleagues to be like him; undisciplined, creative thinkers, impatient with reviewing, concluding and planning. In short, it dawned on him that they should each be allowed to play to their strengths:

- He would be in charge of doing.

- Mr Review would be in charge of reviewing the doing.

- Mr Conclude would be in charge of concluding from the reviewing of the doing.

- Mr Plan would be in charge of planning from the concluding of the reviewing of the doing.

- Then he would be in charge of the doing of the planning from the concluding of the reviewing of the doing.

Dr Do was enormously excited by his insight. It looked to him like the beginnings of a recipe for perpetual motion, perhaps the ultimate impossibility! What a scoop for *The Impossible Objects Company.*

After Dr Do's epiphany, meetings between the four men were much improved with Dr Do, Mr Review, Mr Conclude and Mr Plan each taking the chair for their respective phases of the meeting.

All went well until Dr Do met with an impossible accident. He was playing with the prototype of the latest impossible object which looked like this:

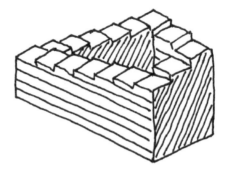

Wondering if it was possible to reach the top, he missed his step and fell to the ground. To have done so was particularly ironic since Mr Plan had already earmarked this as one of the most useful impossible objects they had yet produced. He argued that because the steps didn't lead anywhere, no one would be tempted to climb them and this would be useful in reducing accidents. Mr Plan, as always, had underestimated Dr Do's unquenchable enthusiasm for doing.

While poor Dr Do languished in hospital, doodling on the plaster that encased much of his body, it was necessary for Mr Review, Mr Conclude and Mr Plan to run *The Impossible Objects Company* in his absence. This, of course, meant they had to have meetings. But it quickly became apparent that without Dr Do to do what Mr Plan planned, nothing got done. They just went round in do-less circles until eventually Mr Review ran out of things to review.

The problem was:

- If there was no doing there could be no reviewing.

- If there was no reviewing there could be no concluding.

- If there was no concluding there could be no planning.

- If there was no planning there could be no doing.

Consequently, they'd come to a grinding halt.

Eventually, Mr Review, desperate for something to review, hit upon the idea of reviewing the impasse itself.

After Mr Review had conducted a characteristically thorough review of all the possible whys and wherefores of the impasse, Mr Conclude reached a remarkable conclusion, namely that each of them with their different skills were essential contributors to the whole in the same way that four lots of 25 per cent were essential to 100 per cent. If any 25 per cent was missing, be it the doing, reviewing, concluding or planning, grinding to a halt was inevitable.

This conclusion provoked Mr Plan into planning his most striking plan to date. Like all the best plans it was simple. Mr Plan's plan was that each of them should deliberately practise developing the skills they *weren't* good at so that anyone of them could turn their hands to doing, reviewing, concluding and planning. He called this a contingency plan and argued that it was clearly what they needed to implement in the regrettable absence of Dr Do.

Mr Review mulled this over with considerable trepidation since he was especially fearful of doing anything other than reviewing.

Mr Conclude, whilst appreciating the logic and elegance of the plan, jumped to the conclusion that it would be unlikely he could change his ways. He was a concluder *par excellence* and that was that.

Mr Plan, disappointed by these two adverse reactions, realised that his plan was in jeopardy.

But instead of becoming defensive, he thought of a ploy, which as everyone knows is a mini-plan. It was simply this: he turned to Mr Review and asked him what he proposed to do.

Now, Mr Review couldn't remember the last time anyone had asked him what to do. Doers, like Dr Do, always dealt with the risky business of deciding what to do. After a long silence, Mr Review hesitantly suggested that they should visit Dr Do in hospital, put Mr Plan's plan to him and ask him whether he thought it was worth doing. Upon hearing this, Mr Plan smiled supportively and offered the conclusion that this was, in the circumstances, an admirable suggestion. Mr Conclude, miffed by Mr Plan's audacity in robbing him of the opportunity to reach that conclusion, leapt to his feet and urged his colleagues to do it at once before the visiting hours at the hospital ended, causing an unwelcome delay.

In this way, they had made a tentative start at implementing the plan since:

- Mr Review had been forced to propose a do.

- Mr Plan had seized the opportunity and reached a conclusion.

- And, Mr Conclude, with nothing else to do, had leapt up and done.

Dr Do welcomed them to his bedside even though they interrupted his creation of a potentially promising doodle. Inert, trapped in plaster and an absurd pully contraption that he had redesigned and was going to patent, Dr Do listened to the plan and instantly agreed they should give it a whirl.

And so they did and, as a consequence, any one of them could be absent without things grinding to a halt and the productivity of their meetings rocketed. Each of them could now turn their hands to anything, without friction, with meetings lasting no more than thirty minutes.

And they learnt to be flexible.

- Sometimes they would review, conclude, plan and do.

- Sometimes they would conclude, plan, do and review.

- At other times they would plan, do, review and conclude.

- And sometimes they would do, review, conclude and plan.

These four permutations covered, they were delighted to find, all eventualities. *The Impossible Objects Company* thrived and Mr Conclude concluded that, not only had they mastered the magic of synergetic working, but quite possibly they'd discovered the secret of making the impossible, possible.

And, you'll not be surprised to hear, they all lived happily ever after.

The Helpers

Cornelia was finding her ageing parents hard to help.

'It's obvious they ought to move,' grumbled Cornelia to her long suffering husband, after a long stint in A&E with her mother who had scalded herself draining cabbage into a colander. 'They're in denial. They won't even have a sensible discussion about the idea.'

'They'll come round to it. Give them time,' replied Ben.

'Yes, but only after one of them has fallen down the stairs and broken a hip.'

Jennifer and Eugene, Cornelia's parents, were both in their eighties and stubbornly soldiering on in a house that had outgrown them: Victorian, three flights of stairs, eight bedrooms, over an acre of garden, with two lawns, a herbaceous border, a vegetable patch and a small orchard. Their cleaning lady of fifteen years, Lynn, had recently left to look after her husband who had suffered a stroke. Lynn had been excellent: reliable, willing to turn her hand to anything and, above all, careful with Eugene's priceless collection of blue-on-white china.

Replacing Lynn was proving troublesome. Jennifer had engaged an agency but they sent a different person each week and she had become exasperated having to explain where the cleaning things were, and what to do/not do each time.

'Let me put an advert in the local paper,' Cornelia suggested. 'There must be plenty of Lynn's out there.'

'Thank you, dear. That would be helpful.'

Both Jennifer and Eugene knew, but were loath to admit, that the house, an ideal family home for nearly fifty years, had outgrown them. There were many telltale signs. Jennifer's arthritic fingers could no longer grip things properly. Jars were impossible to open (a gadget from *Granny Get A Grip* had become an essential tool) and, without warning, saucepans had started to misbehave in her hands - hence her recent trip to A&E.

Three flights of stairs were also becoming increasingly daunting, particularly for Jennifer who now relied on the banisters - the same banisters, she recalled, her children used to slide down with yelps of joy - to haul herself up each step.

'You should get a stair lift,' their son had cheerfully suggested on a flying visit. They rarely saw him. He was a merchant banker and lived in New York.

'Ridiculous idea,' Eugene had snorted. 'Too many bends.'

Jennifer's back was also becoming increasingly irksome. She'd always been a keen gardener, growing her own vegetables and tending the herbaceous border, but nowadays bending and, in particular, straightening up again, was painful. Recently she'd admitted defeat and hired a young man called Reg to help with the vegetables and flower borders. He'd been a sergeant in the Ordinance Corps and had an alarming propensity to 'slash and burn'. He'd already scorched the side of the garden shed with a large bonfire that had escalated out of control.

Eugene too, a retired circuit judge, was reluctant to admit that he was starting to find his chores (over the years, their roles had quietly morphed into 'his' and 'hers') too demanding. He'd toppled over recently lugging two heavy shopping bags up the marble steps to the front door. Fortunately, twelve broken eggs (organic) were the only casualties. Until comparatively recently, he'd carefully climbed ladders to clear autumn leaves from the guttering and enjoyed shaping the yew hedges with his electric trimmer. But now Jennifer forbade him to climb ladders and insisted that Reg cut the hedges.

So, with token protests, Eugene had started to relinquish some of his more demanding tasks, stubbornly insisting that mowing the lawns remain an exception. He loved cutting the grass. Over the years he'd developed a special relationship with his mower, a 24-inch Atco, painted in British racing green with red blades. He'd bought the mower when they'd first moved into the house. 'Atco' was picked out in gold lettering on the grass box and a handsome crest confirmed that the mower had won royal approval. Eugene enjoyed imagining the late Queen tottering along behind her faithful 24-inch Atco. When Eugene's mower was collected for its annual service, the mechanic always patted it fondly, muttering, 'Don't make 'em like this anymore'

'Keeps me fit,' Eugene had insisted, sinking into an armchair after an hour of being pulled along by the noisy mower.

'Rubbish! It's absurd for an 86 year old to be cutting the grass,' said Jennifer as she opened the fridge and handed Eugene a can of unopened beer (he was the can-opener). 'You should get Reg to do it.'

'He wouldn't be able to start the mower. There's a knack, you have to get the choke spot on.'

'Surely you could show him how to do it,' Jennifer persisted.

'It's temperamental,' Eugene had insisted, pulling the ring on the beer can, conscious that he must be seen to do it with panache. 'Even if he could start the mower, he'd never get the stripes straight.'

They'd always had help in the house. When the children were small, with Eugene away doing his judging in various parts of the country, Jennifer had employed a series of au pairs, some more willing and able than others. A Japanese au pair, keen to learn English, had spurned the washing line in the orchard and insisted on draping nappies over Eugene's precious hedges. A Swedish au pair had claimed she could drive, but when Jennifer insisted on taking her for a test drive, she'd burst into tears and fled. The police had brought her back later that evening and she'd promptly packed and left. An Italian au pair, a good tennis player, had once returned home after playing on the courts in the local park, minus the children. Fortunately Jennifer found them, unconcerned, playing happily on the climbing frame. Another girl, Lizzy, from France, was moody, sulking for days at the merest hint of a rebuke. Once she'd forgotten to switch off the iron and it had burnt through the ironing board cover setting off the fire alarm (which nobody knew how to switch off). On another occasion she'd slammed a door so hard the glass had shattered.

'I think,' Jennifer had said one evening, 'I'll give up on foreign au pairs and find someone local.'

'Why?' said Eugene, looking up from studying his brief, 'are you expecting they'd be more reliable?'

'Maybe not, but at least it would reduce the communication problems.'

So it was that Jennifer had hired a young woman called Joanne, who'd left school at sixteen and was waiting to start training as a nurse. Unfortunately, despite her being English, problems had quickly become apparent, with Joanne either failing to understand what was asked of her, or wilfully deciding to ignore it.

After a couple of exasperating weeks, Jennifer had admitted defeat. 'You were right, dear. Hiring a local girl hasn't worked. She'll have to go.'

'What's the problem this time?' Eugene had asked, glancing at Jennifer over the top of his spectacles, a habit he'd perfected when sentencing people.

Jennifer, undaunted by the judgemental look, had persisted. 'Either she doesn't listen or she doesn't understand, perhaps both.'

'Maybe something in writing might help clarify things. You know, in plain language, not a brief exactly, more a job description.'

'Perhaps that's worth a try,' Jennifer had half-heartedly conceded. 'But if that doesn't work, that's it, I've done with these youngsters. I'll have to find a proper cleaning woman.'

Jennifer, never having drawn up a job description before, had gone to some trouble to compile a detailed list of duties. She'd given the list to Joanne, asking her to take it home, read it carefully, and come the next day with whatever questions she wanted to ask.

That evening the doorbell had rung and a woman Jennifer hadn't seen before, stood there clutching the precious job description.

'I'm Joanne's mum and I want you to know that she's very upset and she's not coming back. This,' she'd waved the offending document in Jennifer's face, 'is a bloody insult, an *insult!*'

'Oh, I'm sorry, I thought it might help,' Jennifer had said, taken aback.

'*HELP?* It's a fuckin' insult, that's what it is.' And Joanne's mother had ceremoniously torn the job description into tiny pieces, letting them flutter, like confetti, all over the front door step.

Cornelia's advertisement in the local paper had been answered by a young woman called Sally, a vast woman dressed in black keen to chat about her problems (the menopause, a lazy husband who drank too much, children excluded from school, in arrears with the rent, best friend diagnosed with breast cancer) rather than do any work. Another advert to find her replacement had resulted in Judy, undernourished and a diabetic prone to dizzy spells. She'd lasted for six months before being hospitalised with kidney problems.

Undaunted, rather than try another ad in the local paper, Cornelia had asked her WhatsApp mum's group, if they knew of a reliable cleaner. That had resulted in Mrs Palmer (she didn't admit to having a first name), a portly woman of about sixty who addressed Jennifer as 'Mrs Err Umm' and Eugene, on the rare occasions she encountered him, as 'M'lud'. She had a protruding chin with long hairs that Jennifer itched to snip off with her nail scissors. When Mrs Palmer arrived, punctually every Wednesday morning, she'd don an apron, get a bucket and mop out of the cleaning cupboard, and await instructions. Having received them, she'd nod obligingly and say, 'Aw, yuss'.

Jennifer was relieved to find Mrs Palmer was a good worker - quite the best yet - willing to turn her hand to anything, totally trustworthy and content to beaver away with no small talk, only the occasional 'Aw, yusses'.

After a few blissfully satisfactory months, Jennifer asked Mrs Palmer to spring clean the pinewood dresser in the kitchen. Eugene was an enthusiastic collector of blue-on-white china. Over the years, travelling the country in his capacity as a circuit judge, he'd always made time to scour antique shops and prided himself on having picked up many bargains. His collection occupied every plate rack throughout the house, with his latest acquisitions temporarily displayed on the kitchen dresser awaiting cataloguing.

Eugene heard the crash from his study, two floors up. Mrs Palmer, thorough as ever, had decided to clamber up a small step ladder so that she could dust the top of the dresser. Perched on the top step, she suddenly felt unsteady and grabbed the dresser which set off a disastrous chain reaction: the dresser wobbled; two plates become dislodged; Mrs Palmer attempted to catch them; she failed and grabbed the dresser again; it wobbled some more, as if caught in an aftershock; more plates were dislodged; they fell, smashing to pieces on the tiled floor.

Mrs Palmer, ashen, could not be consoled and Jennifer drove her home. The next day a note was pushed through the brass letterbox (the brass still gleaming from Mrs Palmer's weekly polishing). The note, on lined paper apparently torn out of a notebook, was handwritten by Mr Palmer (neither Jennifer nor Eugene had been aware of his existence) and read:

To whom it may concern

Mrs Palmer is sorry she broke your lordship's plates and I regret to inform you that she is no longer able to work for you.

Yours faithfully
Mr Palmer

PS She says you can keep the apron she's left in the cleaning cupboard.

While Eugene busied himself completing an insurance claim, Jennifer conferred yet again with Cornelia.

'Don't worry, I'll ask around,' Cornelia had reassured her mother. But this time she drew a blank, her friends knew of no one suitable. 'Never mind,' Cornelia said, 'I'll try advertising again. You never know, it might work this time.'

The phone rang early on the day of the newspaper's publication and Jennifer answered.

There was a long pause.

Jennifer, suspecting it might be a hoax call, repeated her name.

A voice said, 'Aw, Yuss' and the phone went dead.

The Unintended Consequence

It only took Larry, successful and self-made, a couple of weeks to realised he'd made a silly mistake. It didn't help that once he'd swallowed his pride and told his brother, a business school lecturer and the author of a couple of best-selling management books, what he'd done, he got no sympathy. 'Pity you didn't run that past me. I'd have definitely warned you not to do that.'

'Yes, but now I know it was a mistake, what can I do?'

'And,' added his brother, ignoring the question, 'if you'd bothered to read my latest book, you'd have come across a case study which is uncannily similar to the mess you've got yourself into.'

'OK, OK,' Larry put both his hands up, conceding the point. 'I'll admit I've been too busy to read management books, but I'm asking for your advice on what I should do now.'

Larry's brother shrugged his shoulders. 'Actions have consequences and what's done is done. You're probably going to have to grin and bear it.'

'Well, you're no help,' said Larry miserably. 'I hoped you'd be able to think of something.'

Larry was the owner-manager of a successful laundry specialising in hotel and restaurant linen. He'd left school at 16 after taking his GCSE's and worked in a variety of dead-end jobs before joining the laundry. After his girlfriend, literally the girl next door, became pregnant, he'd married her and, for the first time in his life, he started to apply himself. He went to night school to learn bookkeeping and, over the course of three years, worked his way up to a job in the laundry's office doing the accounts. There he'd watched the business go into slow decline after the owner got early onset dementia and became increasingly forgetful and disoriented.

Larry had weighed up his options: jump ship or stay and do something to reverse the decline. He'd discussed it with his brother who came up with the idea of exploring the possibility of a take-over. 'Nothing ventured, nothing gained,' said his brother. 'Give it a try. You'll probably find the old boy will be relieved to find a way out.' So, ever the opportunist, Larry seized the initiative and struck an advantageous deal with the owner and his wife - a tapered management buyout, with Larry paying the asking price in instalments over a six-year period.

Over the five years since the buyout, Larry had turned the ailing business into a profitable operation. He'd invested in new equipment and engaged a marketing agency to promote the laundry's services. Seven days a week, a fleet of vans set off on their respective rounds, delivering clean, and collecting, dirty linen. There were two alternating teams of drivers, one covering Mondays to Thursdays and another Fridays to Sundays, each shift starting at 8am and finishing at 4pm.

Larry often stood at the window of his first-floor office watching the vans come and go, feeling proud of his achievements.

He'd not excelled at school, finding it uninspiring and boring. The only subjects he'd really enjoyed were geography and art. In the main, his teachers despaired of him, comparing him unkindly with his elder brother who had been a high flyer and became head boy before progressing to university. Larry's teachers were surprised when he got a clutch of reasonable GCSE grades but, he suspected, relieved that he opted to leave school and not proceed to the sixth form.

One day the driver's rep, Joe, came to see Larry. Joe was a large man with a protruding beer belly, but his most distinguishing characteristic was his ginger hair, swept straight back as if he was walking into the teeth of a gale. The two men knew each other well and chatted for a while about football, both being Arsenal supporters, before Larry asked, 'So, what do you want, Joe? A pay rise for the drivers I suppose?'

'How'd you work that out?' teased Joe. 'Are you clairvoyant or something?'

Larry smiled. 'Come on then, spit it out.'

Joe went on to put his case for an 8% increase to the van driver's hourly rate. It was predictable stuff: the rising cost of living, no wage increase for the past two years, competitive hourly rates being offered by local supermarkets, and so on.

'Well, said Larry, leaning back in his reclining chair, 'you wouldn't expect me to agree to that without giving it careful consideration. I need to do some calculations to see how it would impact our margins and think through the implications for other staff.'

Joe smirked. 'Your precious bottom line. I'll leave it with you then.'

That evening Larry attended a Round Table meeting where,

in addition to downing lots of beer, the members listened to a guest speaker who took as his theme the Round Table motto: adopt, adapt, improve. The speaker waxed lyrical about the need to be adventurous and embrace new ideas. Larry walked home, slightly tipsy, enthused by what he'd heard and feeling increasingly bold. As he reached his front door and fumbled for the key, a novel idea struck him. He smiled to himself and could hear his brother's voice saying, 'nothing ventured, nothing gained'.

He swayed slightly as he joined his wife, Sue, on the sofa. She was watching the TV, an item on *Newsnight* about rising inflation and its impact on small businesses, but turned the sound down and gave Larry a kiss on his cheek.

'My, you've obviously had a good time, you reek of beer! How did the meeting go?'

'I only had a couple of pints,' Larry said defensively. 'It was quite interesting actually. Made me think I ought to be more adventurous and, hey presto, I've had an idea that avoids giving the drivers a pay increase.'

'Oh yes, and what's that? Sack them all and get the customers to collect and deliver their own laundry?'

Larry smiled. 'Well, I'd admit it's not as novel as that. No, my idea is to leave them on the same pay but reduce their hours.'

Sue looked puzzled. 'And why would they agree to that?'

'Simple,' beamed Larry, 'they'd be able to supplement their income by getting second jobs.'

Sue looked doubtful. 'Well, best sleep on it, dear, and see if it seems such a good idea in the morning.'

'Yes, of course. But I'm inclined to give it a whirl.'

'A whirl?'

'Yes, a trial period. An experiment. A toe in the water, nothing too risky.'

'How about running it past your brother first?' Sue suggested.

'No, I need to learn to be bolder, to stand on my own two feet. I can't keep running to him asking for advice.' Larry paused, watching a politician he didn't recognise being interviewed on the telly before adding, 'Anyway, he's an academic. I'm dealing with the real world.'

A few days later Larry met with Joe again.

'Thanks for coming Joe. As I promised, I've given your request due consideration and I'm afraid I can't agree to an 8% increase to the hourly rate. As I feared, it would be too much of a stretch and, as I'm sure you'll understand, I can't do anything that might jeopardise the stability of the company.'

'Well, I suppose that comes as no surprise,' said Joe, looking glum. 'You and your precious bloody bottom line. Still, I have to warn you that the drivers will take it badly. They're expecting a pay increase.'

'Never mind,' said Larry, undaunted, 'I have an alternative proposition to put to you that I think the drivers will find attractive.'

'Go on,' said Joe, looking far from convinced, 'What have you dreamt up that's better than a pay rise? I'm all ears.'

'Instead of giving the drivers a pay increase, I propose a change to their working practices.' Larry paused momentarily, as if announcing the winner of a Bafta award. 'How about reducing their hours? Same pay for less hours.'

Joe looked puzzled. 'Tell me more.'

'Simple, just like it says on the tin, when a driver has finished his round he can clock off. I've noticed how they often hang around chatting waiting for 4 o'clock.'

'Ah, I see,' said Joe, his face momentarily lighting up. 'You're proposing a finish-and-go scheme.'

'If that's what it's called, then yes.'

Joe looked incredulous. 'Just let me check I've got this right. You're saying the drivers can go after they've finished their rounds?'

'Exactly,' Larry sat back, looking pleased with himself. 'An attractive proposition, eh? Same pay, less hours.'

Joe crossed his arms so that they rested above his generous stomach, like a baby seal on a rock ledge. 'Well, if you're sure. Let me put it to the drivers but I can't promise anything.'

'Let's give it a whirl. Nothing ventured, nothing gained.' Larry leapt up and looked out of the window. 'Let's try it for a six-month period and see how it goes.'

The next day Joe returned looking suspiciously cheerful and told Larry that he'd managed to persuade the drivers to agree to the change to their working practices. Larry shook Joe's hand enthusiastically. 'Well done! You'll not regret it.'

Joe smiled as if he was holding something back. 'Anything to avoid shelling out more money, eh?'

After a couple of weeks, an angry telephone call from the general manager of a large hotel was the first indication that something was amiss. Larry knew the caller well. Over the years he'd made a point of getting to know his customers, visiting them regularly to check all was well.

'Larry, your bloody driver refused to wait for the linen this morning. He arrived early, dropped off the clean stuff and buggered off without picking up the dirty. Just swore when he heard it wasn't ready and drove off. We expected him to come back, but he hasn't. The stuff's still waiting for collection. What the hell's going on?'

Larry, apologised profusely, and promised to despatch a van immediately.

Over the next few days, more complaints came in about drivers being rude and in too much of a hurry. 'This hasn't happened before,' said one restaurant owner. 'Your drivers have always had time to stop for a coffee and a chat.'

Larry summoned Joe to a meeting. 'I'm afraid it's becoming apparent that the finish-and-go scheme has unforeseen snags. I'm getting complaints from customers that your drivers are being discourteous and in too much of a hurry.'

'Just teething problems,' said Joe, not looking in the least surprised. 'Only to be expected. It's early days. We need more time for the drivers to adapt to the new arrangement.'

'Well,' said Larry, 'in the meantime, I'm the one who's taking the flack. And there's another problem. The garage that services the vans is reporting an increase in bodywork damage - nothing major yet, just dents and scrapes. It's obvious that the drivers are being careless. I think we should agree to halt the experiment.'

'Experiment? Who said it was an experiment?' Joe said rather belligerently.

'We agreed to a six-month trial, so in my book that's an experiment,' Larry replied gloomily.

Joe stood up rather abruptly. 'That's as may be, but I think you'll find it well-nigh impossible to revert to the old arrangement. Some of the drivers have already found second jobs. What's done is done.'

Joe left leaving Larry to reflect ruefully that his brother had used exactly the same expression: what's done is done. His brother's latest book, *Anticipating Consequences,* lay unopened on the windowsill behind him.

The Delivery

'If I were you, I'd take it to the dump,' Janet had said, busy chopping up carrots. 'It's up to you. Just saying.'

'Someone might want it. I think I'll put it outside and see if there are any takers,' Nicholas had replied.

'Up to you, but I'd dump it.'

Manoeuvring the filing cabinet out of his garden office was more of a struggle than Nicholas had expected. Three steps down to the crazy paving path, then wrapping it in an old blanket and lifting it, corpse-like, onto his wheelbarrow. Then a wobbly journey the length of the garden, past the pond, through the garden gate (very tricky, nearly lost it), up the gravel drive to the pavement.

Having got there, Nicholas left the grey, slightly dented, filing cabinet with a note taped to the top drawer saying:

Hello
I'm homeless and trying to get my life back together. If you can give me a good home, please take me.

Nicholas was particularly chuffed with this witty note, produced after a number of iterations. He'd drafted, but rejected, curt ones such as, '*Help yourself - no longer wanted*' and '*Serviceable filing cabinet, please take*'. And he'd tried persuasive ones such as, '*Very useful filing cabinet. It fits snuggly into a corner and the 4-drawers run smoothly. Admittedly, it has a few dents, but they add to its charm. And it's free!*' He'd also tried emotional ones along the lines of, '*I need a hug. Please take me if you can provide a loving home*'.

'A ridiculous waste of time,' Janet had pronounced. 'Someone's bound to report you to the council for obstructing the pavement. Just take it to the dump and have done with it.'

'It's worth a try. It's not doing any harm,' Nicholas had replied.

'Suppose a blind person collides with it. You'd be liable.'

'I'm not sure you can say blind anymore. You probably have to say 'visually challenged'. Anyway, that's not very likely. I'll take my chances,' said Nicholas, with little conviction.

After the first day, Nicholas was disappointed to find the filing cabinet was exactly where he'd left it and that a passing dog had peed against the bottom drawer. He took the cabinet in for the night and washed it. He was amazed to find a couple of cigarette ends and the wrapper from a crisp packet in the top drawer.

The next morning, Nicholas put the filing cabinet out again, where it stoically remained all day, baking in the late September sunshine. This time, when he took it in for the night, there was a banana skin left on the top and someone had scribbled 'Fuck off' on his precious notice.

On the third day, Nicholas had decided it would be his last

attempt, he put the cabinet out once more with a fresh 'I'm homeless' notice written with a blue, permanent marker.

At lunchtime the doorbell rang and Janet opened the front door to find an overweight woman, dressed in a loose-fitting black dress, standing on the doorstep. She was holding the notice from the filing cabinet.

'Is this yours?' she asked brusquely.

'No,' said Janet, 'it's my husband's.'

'Does he want anything for it?'

'I don't think so. Wait, I'll call him.'

Nicholas, still eating the remnants of a cheese sandwich, came to the door. 'Are you interested in the filing cabinet?' he asked hopefully.

'Yes. Do you want anything for it?'

'Lord no! I've had it for years, it's not worth anything. I was going to take it to the dump this evening if no one wanted it.'

'Can you deliver it?' the woman asked.

'Well,' said Nicholas, somewhat taken aback, 'I was expecting someone to take it.'

'I can't take it. I don't have a car,' the woman announced, as if it were Nicholas's fault that she was without transport.

'I suppose it depends where you live,' said Nicholas warily, feeling he was standing at the top of a slippery slope.

'Only a mile or so away,' came the answer.

'*What*!' Janet exclaimed when, sheepishly, Nicholas told her he'd agreed to deliver the cabinet. 'You're barmy. If she wants it, surely she can arrange for someone to collect it.'

Nicholas knew Janet was right (she was *always* right!). 'It won't take long. It's not far to go,' he said defensively.

After lunch, Nicholas loaded the filing cabinet into the back of his Volvo Estate. This took far longer than he'd expected because he couldn't work out how to release the drawers from their runners. Eventually he discovered the knack and the filing cabinet lay on its back, surrounded by its dismembered drawers.

The drawers rattled against the side of the cabinet as Nicholas drove gingerly over a number of speed bumps on his way to the address the woman had given him. He found the house, a narrow, terraced house, with a small overgrown front garden. He drove past slowly in search of somewhere to park. Eventually he squeezed into a parking place by a notice saying, 'Residents Only'.

He walked back along the street and rang the front door bell. As he waited, he wondered why all the curtains were drawn and watched butterflies fluttering happily on the rampant buddleias. After a longish wait, the woman appeared. Nicholas guessed she was about sixty. She still wore the same black dress, but now her lips glistened with freshly applied red lipstick and she wore no shoes. 'Well, where's my cabinet?' she demanded, looking at Nicholas standing there empty-handed.

'I'm parked along the street,' said Nicholas, feeling ridiculously apologetic. 'Couldn't get any closer. Is there anyone who can help me unload?'

'Afraid not. And I can't help, I suffer from angina.'

As Nicholas eased the cabinet out of the Volvo, scraping the back bumper, he could hear Janet's voice saying 'you're barmy'. He left the drawers in the Volvo and 'walked' the cabinet along the pavement, pausing occasionally to regain his breath. Tall sunflowers in a garden he passed seemed to be nodding to him sympathetically.

When at last Nicholas reached the terraced house, he was surprised to find the woman had vanished and the front door was shut. He knocked and stood there, wondering again why all the curtains were drawn.

The door eventually opened. 'Ah, it's you.'

'Yes,' said Nicholas, needlessly. 'Where do you want me to put it?'

'Upstairs, in the back bedroom.'

'*Upstairs*? Can you ask a neighbour or someone to help?'

'No, I've only moved in recently. Anyway, they're out at work.' He heard Janet's voice again: you're barmy.

Nicholas eased the cabinet over an awkward ledge and into a narrow hallway. As his eyes adjusted to the gloom, he was confronted with a chaotic scene. A bicycle blocked his path and, beyond it, stood an oak bookcase, its shelves haphazardly stacked with files.

'See why I want a filing cabinet?' the woman asked. Nicholas assumed it was a rhetorical question.

Nicholas lifted the filing cabinet back out into the overgrown front garden. Then he reversed the bicycle out, the pedals catching his ankle. Then he moved the files from the bookcase onto a table in the gloomy front room. Finally, he manoeuvred the bookcase out into the garden where it joined the bicycle and cabinet. Gentle rain started to fall.

'May I look at the stairs?' asked Nicholas.

'Sure,' said the woman obligingly. 'I'm afraid you'll need to move a few things.'

The stairs, narrow with a steep bend half way up, had stacks of papers on each step, some with used coffee mugs balanced on top.

Aghast, Nicholas asked needlessly, 'Is this stuff all yours?'

'Yes, I've just moved in and I'm still sorting things out.'

There was that voice again: you're barmy.

Nicholas cleared the stairs, adding to the chaos in the pokey front room. Then he eased the cabinet along the hall and, one step at a time, slowly ascended the narrow stairway, pausing on each step to regain his breath. The tight corner half way up proved, as Nicholas had feared, a major problem. The cabinet stuck, jammed against the wall, and Nicholas was forced to retreat and change the angle of the cabinet before he was able to ease it forward again.

The woman watched, temporarily (perhaps permanently!) trapped on the landing, muttering, 'I can't believe we're doing this'. Nicholas thought, but did not say, 'we?'. When the cabinet reached the top of the stairs, she leant forward in a futile gesture of help, her black dress gaping alarmingly to reveal pendulous, white breasts.

Eventually, Nicholas eased the cabinet into a chaotic back bedroom. It only remained for him to retrieve the four drawers, one at a time, from the Volvo. Fitting the drawers onto their runners proved tricky. After a struggle he managed the first three but the top drawer refused to cooperate and, as he wrestled with it, a searing pain shot through his back. He abandoned the skewwhiff drawer, staggered down the stairs, on the way passing a chunk of plaster the cabinet must have gouged out of the wall. He limped past the bookshelves and bicycle standing forlornly in the front garden. When he reached the Volvo he found a parking ticket on the windscreen.

He drove home carefully, the shooting pains in his back worsening with each speed bump.

By the time he got back, he'd seized up completely and sat in the Volvo wondering how he was going to get out of the driving seat. Eventually he phoned Janet on his mobile.

'Where are you?' she asked. 'Whatever could have taken you so long?'

The Handmade Shoes

Dear Mrs Smeaton

Nice to talk on the phone and thanks for giving me your email address. As promised, I'm attaching scans of the letters your father wrote to my father 25 years ago. As I told you, I found them in a tin trunk along with lots of other letters my late father had kept. I'm also attaching the letter you wrote on 3 May 1999 that you've probably forgotten after all this time.

I hope you find the correspondence amusing. I have no idea why things went wrong. All the other letters in the trunk were testimonials from satisfied customers - my father was always very proud of those.

Best wishes
Yasmin Marangoz (nee Bagzibagli)

The Poplars
Shortcut Lane
Lewes
E Sussex
England

3 September 1998

Mahmut Bagzibagli Esq
Shoemaker of Distinction
52 Ataturk Street
Kyrenia
Northern Cyprus

Dear Mr Bagzibagli

I wonder if you remember me? I visited your shop a couple of weeks ago when my wife and I were holidaying on your beautiful island. You were kind enough to greet us with cups of tea and little squares of Turkish Delight. While we drank tea you invited us to peruse a binder containing handwritten testimonials from famous people - a delightful, but unexpected welcome. I must admit it was a little overwhelming - nothing like that has happened to me before when visiting a shoe shop. Reading all those testimonials from film stars, diplomats, politicians and entrepreneurs was rather humbling!

Eventually my wife gave me a nudge and I plucked up the courage to ask if you'd kindly make me a pair of sandals. On reflection, I think you probably ignored this because asking for sandals, not shoes, was an insult (please accept my sincere apologies for any offence I unwittingly caused). I should explain that I particularly wanted sandals in order to replace the ones that broke on the long climb (well, clamber really!) up the rough steps to Saint Hillarion Castle (wonderful views, well worth the effort!). Anyway, if asking for sandals was a faux pas, you didn't appear to take umbrage. On the contrary, you smiled graciously and showed us a letter from Sean Connery where he waxed lyrical about the shoes you'd made for him. Underneath his signature, he'd written 'Bond, James Bond' - a nice touch.

The impasse might have continued indefinitely but my wife rescued me - she's much better at handling these situations than I am! She thanked you for tea and said we had to go. You, courteous as ever, didn't remonstrate or seek to detain us, but bowed and opened the door for us. We stepped outside into the sunshine, emptyhanded but for your business card.

In the two weeks that have elapsed since returning home (we stayed at the Dome Hotel, it was the concierge there who recommended we pay you a visit), I've been thinking about those impressive testimonials written by the Great and the Good. I cannot of course claim to be in their league, but nonetheless I'm writing to ask if you'd make me a pair of black shoes and post them to me.

Please advise on the next steps (no pun intended!). You will obviously need measurements and perhaps payment in advance. I look forward to hearing from you. Should you need to telephone the number is 01273 228143.

Yours sincerely
Robin Goodfellow

14 October 1998

Dear Mr Mr Bagzibagli

I wonder if you received my letter dated 3 September asking if you'd make me a pair of black shoes? I just tried to telephone you but there was no reply (quite possibly I was using the wrong code for Northern Cyprus).

I appreciate that it would have been far more convenient for all concerned if I'd asked you to make me a pair of shoes (not sandals!) when we visited your shop in August. You would no doubt have used your tape measure (the one dangling round your neck like a doctor wearing a stethoscope) to take careful measurements, etc. However, since I am now over two thousand miles away, I enclose a sheet of paper providing the measurements I'm assuming you require. You'll see that it includes drawings of the imprints of both my feet (my wife kindly did the outlines).

I'm anticipating that you'll doubt the accuracy of these measurements because my feet are exceptionally large - size 15. You'll also note from the enclosed drawings that my feet are very wide. Everyone says I missed my true vocation, I should have been a policeman! My feet grew to this size by the time I was sixteen. I have large hands too - at school people often complained that the combination of large feet *and* hands gave me an unfair advantage in competitive swimming races, particularly the breaststroke, and it's true that I won many cups comparatively effortlessly.

Still, I digress. How would you like me to pay, in advance or will you enclose an invoice when you despatch the shoes? Please be sure to add something to cover the postage and I'll send a cheque by return.

Don't hesitate to ask if anything isn't clear and apologies again that requesting you to make me a pair of shoes (just a reminder, black please) is an afterthought.

Yours sincerely
Robin Goodfellow

1 November 1998

Dear Mr Bagzibagli
Further to my letter of 14 October, which I hope you received safely, it occurs to me that you might require a downpayment. I'm therefore enclosing a cheque for £60. Please let me know if this is insufficient and, if so, I'll send more by return.

Perhaps you'd kindly confirm when I might expect the shoes to arrive? By Christmas would be lovely but I'm loath to pressurise you in any way. In my business life (alas, a distant memory!) I always found harrying people to be counterproductive.

Yours sincerely
Robin Goodfellow

5 January 1999

Dear Mr Bagzibagli
Thank you so much for the shoes, which I can confirm arrived safely on Christmas Eve (splendid timing!). Thank you also for enclosing an invoice covering the balance due.

I must admit that since writing to you in November, and not hearing anything further from you prior to the arrival of the shoes, I was worried that my letters and cheque might have gone astray or that, for some reason, you'd decided not to proceed with my order for a pair of black shoes.

Anyway, I've hesitated to write earlier (and to send another cheque) because I've been in something of a quandary. To be frank, it's a little awkward, especially as you'll be expecting, not only payment, but also a glowing testimonial to add to your collection. The fact of the matter is that the shoes you have sent are too tight. It's a struggle to squeeze my feet into them and walking in the shoes is, well, agony.

I'm sorry to be the bearer of bad news. Perhaps you misread the measurements I sent or, more probably, assumed the outlines my wife drew were inaccurate? Is it conceivable that when you studied the dimensions you were in disbelief and consciously (or unconsciously) made adjustments? Anyway, whatever the explanation, I'm sorry to have to tell you that the shoes are too narrow.

What would you like me to do? Return the shoes or give them to a charity shop? I have a grandson who has big feet (a chip off the old block!) but he tried them on and they are too small for him too. Please advise on the best course of action.

Again, I'm sorry to have to write this letter conveying what will obviously be disappointing news. I'll wait to hear further from you.

Yours sincerely
Robin Goodfellow

PS Have you kept a note of my telephone number? In case not, it is 01273 228143.

14 March 1999

Dear Mr Bagzibagli

Thank you for sending a second pair of shoes but I'm sorry to tell you they are too big, *much* too big actually (a novel experience for me, never before having encountered shoes that are too large!). I have experimented by wearing three pairs of socks but I fear it would need five or six pairs to fill the void.

I am at a loss to know how to proceed. Naturally I would rather not pay for shoes that don't fit, but I'm conscious that you have invested your time and expertise in building (is that the right expression, do shoes get built?) two pairs of superb handmade shoes. I think it best if I put the shoes aside until I hear what you'd like me to do with them.

The options would seem to be:

1. Return the shoes to you (but what is the likelihood of you having customers with feet the right size? I suppose American holidaymakers might be the best bet).
2. See if I can sell the shoes (alas, a long shot) and, if so, send you the proceeds.
3. Give the shoes to a charity shop. (I'd feel a bit guilty about this since they are as unlikely to encounter people with the right sized feet as you are.)
4. Throw the shoes away. (We have a municipal dump fairly close by, but I'm not sure I could bring myself to toss two pairs of brand new - indeed, magnificent - shoes into the general waste skip).

Perhaps you can suggest other possibilities? Please advise. I'm sure you'll agree that this is all very regrettable since, as you may recall, when my wife and I visited your shop last August, my original request was for you to make me a pair of sandals to replace the ones that broke whilst climbing those wretched steps.

Yours sincerely
  Robin Goodfellow

3 May 1999

Dear Mr Bagzibagli

I am Robin Goodfellow's daughter and I'm writing on his behalf to acknowledge the safe arrival of the parcel you have sent (what beautiful stamps, I have a son who collects them and he is very chuffed). My father would write himself but I'm sorry to tell you that he became very agitated when your parcel arrived and, before he could open it, suffered a stroke. My mother called an ambulance and he was rushed to hospital. He is home now and making a slow recovery.

In order to avoid causing him any further distress, I have opened the parcel and found the sandals you have kindly made for him. In the circumstances, I'm sure you'll understand that my father does not require any sandals. He is in his seventies and since his stroke, remains very unsteady on his feet.

I am therefore returning the sandals forthwith.

Yours sincerely
  Jennifer Smeaton (Mrs)

PS My eldest son has big feet (like his grandfather) and he tried the sandals on, but I'm sorry to tell you they were too big for him.

The Special Offer

I'd been researching my family tree, on and off, for some time. Not diligently, just as the mood took me. So when the special offer arrived, I admit I didn't give it enough consideration. Not nearly enough. My reaction was, 'Oh, that could be interesting'. I paid the asking fee of £70 plus VAT and opted to meet my great-grandmother who had died in 1923.

I should have given my choice much more thought. Afterall, if Ancestry.co.uk were to be believed, the special offer to meet an antecedent was just that: special, a one-off. I've no excuse. The email made it clear that it was a 'once in a lifetime opportunity'. I was, as usual, too damned casual.

I could, for example, have opted to meet my maternal grandfather who had died just before I was born. He, fascinatingly, had set fire to himself whilst smoking in bed. Or, better still, I could have chosen to meet his father, my great-grandfather, who, apparently, had cut his throat with one of those razors you see in old gangster films.

But I chose to meet my great-grandmother, mainly because, even though she had died, aged 68, only fifteen years before I was born, the information I had about her was scant. My father must have known her well, she was his granny after all, but never spoke about her. My aunt mentioned her a few times in passing, but only to tell me she was a tall, gaunt woman, always dressed in black, who'd had 'a hard life' after her husband died.

Intriguing. But, like a clot, I didn't quiz either my father or aunt and now they are both dead. It occurs to me that I could have opted to meet one of them to ask all the questions I failed to ask when they were alive. Too late, and I didn't see an 'edit' facility on the Ancestry website so perhaps it wouldn't have been possible to change my mind.

So, Harriet, my great-grandmother it was. I consoled myself that this wasn't a bad choice since she was such a shadowy figure. I've searched the family photos I've inherited but there are none of her. I have faded, stiffly posed, studio photos of my other great-grandparents, and even of my great-great-grandparents, but Harriet is conspicuous by her absence. The chance to put flesh on the bones (sorry, couldn't resist it!) and meet Harriet was therefore intriguing.

As the date for the meeting approached, I made a few notes about what I wanted to ask her and wondered, in a daydreamy sort of way, how things might go. It's easy to assume you'd find meeting up with a dead relative fascinating and enjoyable. But the more I thought about it, the more I realised it could be awkward. Perhaps they'd resent your prying. They might even be annoyed at being disturbed, like waking someone from a deep sleep. You might be shocked to find that, other than your genetic relationship, you had little in common.

The offer from Ancestry.co.uk included some guidelines, some Do's and Don'ts:

- DO arrange to meet on neutral territory where they won't feel daunted or ill-at-ease.

- DO be respectful towards your ancestor.

- DO listen attentively.

- DO thank them profusely for returning to meet you.

- DON'T comment on their appearance or dress.

- DON'T bear grudges or be judgmental. In particular, don't dwell on mistakes you think they might have made when living.

- DON'T argue or correct them even if you believe something they tell you isn't accurate.

- DON'T try to detain them over the allotted time of one hour maximum.

- DON'T pester them to tell you about the afterlife. They are instructed not to talk about life after death.

I ticked the box confirming that I'd read these guidelines and another box agreeing to abide by them.

With the first 'do' in mind, I decided against inviting Harriet to my home because I thought it might be overwhelming for her. I live in a large Edwardian house and I know from various census returns that she'd spent her life living in rundown areas of Oxford, slums mostly, places that have long since been demolished or gentrified. So, I opted for neutral ground and arranged to meet Harriet in a pub in Little Clarendon Street, close to where she used to live. I'm guessing she knows this pub of old. I forgot to mention that my aunt had told me that

Harriet was a heavy drinker and that her son, when the poor little blighter was only ten, used to search for her in pubs and beg her to come home. I hoped that meeting Harriet in a familiar environment would help to put her at her ease.

Naturally I've done some homework in preparation, but the information I have is scant. I've seen an online copy of her marriage certificate, dated 13 November 1875. She was 20, a domestic servant, and the groom, John, 22. He is described as a 'college servant', a gardener at New College. They both signed the marriage certificate with crosses, not signatures. I have also seen records from a census, so I know where they were living when he died and where she moved to afterwards. Harriet's husband died of pneumonia at the age of 33, leaving her with five children. I remember her oldest, Charles, my grandfather, since I was eleven when he died. He was a tall, grumpy man, and, of course, it never occurred to me to ask him anything about his childhood (or even to imagine he had had one!). Perhaps I should have opted to meet him.

Not much to go on; less than meeting someone on a blind date!

The day for our meeting duly arrived and I felt unexpectedly apprehensive. In the absence of any photographs, I wondered how I'd recognise her.

I got to the pub in good time, chose a seat in a corner with a commanding view of the entrance, and waited anxiously, sipping a pint of bitter. It occurred to me that I didn't really know how she'd arrive. Perhaps there'd be a loud whooshing noise and Harriet would step out of a Tardis.

After a short while, an old woman shuffled in, using a walking stick. It was obviously her, in her sixties (but looking older) and dressed in black. I stood up to greet her, uncertain whether to give her a hug or shake her hand, trying to recall whether there was anything in the guidelines about touching.

I'd decided to record our conversation on my phone. I thought that if I sat there taking copious notes she might find it off-putting. Here is our recorded conversation, typed out verbatim.

'You must be Harriet. Thanks for coming. I'm Paul.'

'Pleased to meet you, I'm sure.'

'I thought you might have had second thoughts about meeting me.'

'I did, but in the end I couldn't resist the invitation to meet you. I was curious because I never knew I had a great-grandson.'

'Well, I suppose you couldn't have known because I was born fifteen years after you'd died. Or do you get to know what's happening beyond the grave, as it were?'

'I don't think I'm allowed to answer that. I was given strict instructions.'

'Oh yes, sorry, I shouldn't have asked that. I think you know this pub?'

'Yes, I used to pass it every day on my way to work.'

'I saw that you once lived in Little Clarendon Street.'

'No, we lived not far away, rented accommodation in Beaumont Street, but I used to walk past here on my way to work at the University Press.'

'Really? I never knew you worked there. Would you like a drink?'

'Thanks. I thought you'd never ask. A sherry please.'

I paused the recording while I went to the bar. While I waited for my turn to be served, I worried she might change her mind and disappear. I glanced over to where she was sitting. I thought she looked ill-at-ease, gazing down at her hands. She was twiddling her fingers as if she were surprised they were able to move. I resolved to do more to put her at her ease. Perhaps the sherry would help.

The recording continues.

'May I ask what you did at the University Press? Were you a cleaner?'

'A cleaner? Why ever would you think that?'

'Because I thought you and your husband were illiterate. I saw an online copy of your marriage certificate and both you and your husband had signed it with crosses.'

'Nonsense! What does online mean? You must have been looking at someone else's marriage certificate.'

'Sorry. I forgot you couldn't know about accessing documents electronically.'

'I'm afraid you've lost me there.'

'Please forget I ever said it. May I ask about your husband? I believe he died when he was only 33. That must have been a very difficult time.'

'No, that's not quite right. He was 38 and I was 36. He left me with four surviving children and you're right, it was a struggle but my parents were very helpful. I couldn't have kept my job but for them. The Press were good too. They kept me on with reduced hours.'

'I thought that when your husband died you were expecting your fifth child?'

'No, Harry was born in January and John died in July. He died of pneumonia, a common cause of death in our times. He got a chest infection and couldn't shake it off.'

'I'm sorry. I suppose he was vulnerable, what with working outside in all weathers and, of course, penicillin hadn't been discovered.'

'I don't know anything about Penny Sillen or what she has to do with anything and my John didn't work outside. He was a clerk in the bursar's office at Trinity.'

'Really? Sorry, I must have got that wrong. So when he died you were left with five children and the youngest was only six months old. That must have been really tough.'

'No, four children. My eldest, Charles, was ten, Emily nine, Kate seven and baby Harry.'

'That's strange. Had you already lost a child?'

'No. Why would you think that? Lots of children used to die in infancy in my day but thankfully we were spared that ordeal.'

'Would you like another sherry?'

'Thank you, I wouldn't mind.'

I paused the recording and went back to the bar. I was puzzled. She was correcting everything I asked. Clearly my homework, such as it was, had either been careless or the few documents I had located online were inaccurate. I decided to abandon the remaining questions I'd planned to ask: about what became of her children, what she remembered of my father as a child, about life in Oxford during WW1. I returned with a sherry for Harriet and another beer for me. I continued the recording.

'What's that gadget you keep fiddling with?'

'It's called a smart phone. Perhaps I should have asked if you minded me recording our conversation. I'm writing some notes on the family history for my grandchildren and naturally

I want to include information about you, preferably with a photograph too.'

'No photographs please. I always refused to appear in family photos and I'm not going to start now.'

'That's a shame. Still, I might draw you from memory after you've gone.'

'Suit yourself, but I must insist on no photographs. Anyway, I don't expect a ghost can be photographed.'

'I'd have taken a chance but a sketch will suffice. May I ask why you're buried in Sandford-on-Thames and not in Oxford?'

'So far as I'm aware I'm buried with my husband in the Wolvercote cemetery on the Banbury Road.'

'Are you quite sure? I've visited your grave and read the head-stone. Look, here's the photo I took. It's not too clear because of all the ivy. I plan to go back soon with secateurs and sort it out.'

'Well, that's kind of you but that's not our grave.'

'Not your grave? Really?'

'No. My name is Harriet Forster, not Foster.'

I'm asking Ancestry.co.uk for a refund and for the 'once in a lifetime opportunity' to become a 'twice in a life time opportunity'. Let's hope they send the right person next time.

The List

For some time he'd been vaguely aware that something wasn't quite right. Duncan and his wife, Julie, had been married for 16 years. They'd been teenage sweethearts having met at their co-educational secondary school. Everyone who knew them assumed they'd get married and, sure enough, when Duncan had finished university (English at Cambridge) and got his first job (writing marketing literature for a big multi-national), they obliged.

They honeymooned in Devon at a hotel Duncan knew well from childhood holidays. They expected to have children but, as the years passed, none came along and gradually they settled to an orderly, childless existence: routine and humdrum.

It was therefore a surprise when, at breakfast, shortly after his fortieth birthday, Duncan suddenly announced he'd made a list.

'A list? What sort of list?' Julie asked, a spoon-full of porridge hovering mid-way between her bowl and her mouth.

'Well,' he said sheepishly, 'it's a silly list.'

'A silly list? Let me guess, you've made a bucket list.'

'Not a bucket list exactly, but I suppose there are similarities. I've had it for a couple of days but I hesitated to show you because I knew you'd probably laugh.'

Duncan was an organised man, a slave to his daily routines. For example, when shaving he always used the same shaving gel, the same Gillette disposable razors, pulling the same faces in the same mirror at more or less the same time each morning. After dressing (always in a blue shirt, grey jumper and black corduroys), he would go for a brisk walk, following the same route, pausing only to buy a newspaper each morning (always *The Guardian*) and a banana for Julie. He was invariably served by the same ginger-haired woman, always exchanging a few words with her about the weather.

Then over breakfast (always two shredded wheat, with a sprinkling of seeds and some raisins, in his favourite bowl) he'd settle down to read his newspaper. He always read the leader first, followed by the articles in the comments section. At precisely 10am he would retire to his study where he'd write a thousand words, emerging at precisely 12.45 to prepare a light lunch (always a bowl of soup with two pieces of wholemeal bread) and watch the 1 o'clock news on television.

He was slightly more flexible in the afternoons, preferring to work for a couple of hours until 4.30, at which time he'd welcome Julie home and they'd have a cup of tea and a biscuit (or two, he had a weakness for ginger biscuits, never dunked).

Julie, a teacher at the local primary school, was inclined to be more adventurous than her husband (not difficult!) but she too had her routines and foibles. For example, she always folded sheets and towels in a particular way, kept her shoes in the boxes they originally came in, could never throw away carrier bags and had accumulated a vast collection of cookery books full of recipes she never used.

One day, whilst travelling on a train, Duncan picked up a discarded Metro newspaper and flicked through the pages skimming various items, including his horoscope. The Sagittarius paragraph read:

Do you feel you're drifting, stuck in a rut, not having enough excitement in your life? Today's lunar phase should inspire you to look at new interests, to become more adventurous. This could be an excellent time to unleash your latent spirit of adventure. Seize the day, you'll not regret it!

Even though he disparaged such trivia, he was surprised to find these words unsettling. Until now he'd been content with his lot. Indeed, when unexpected events forced him to depart from his cosy routines - funerals, power cuts, icy pavements for example - he always felt irritable: thrown off-balance, out of kilter.

So, Duncan, despite himself, fell to wondering what it would be like to be more adventurous. He even found himself wondering what it would be like to be married to someone else. His late mother had married three times and, having outlived all her husbands, finishing up co-habiting with the village handyman. One of her little jokes was that he'd certainly come in handy and, after she died, he'd risen to the occasion by building her a plywood coffin with her favourite flowers stencilled on the sides.

Duncan had often been on the brink of quizzing his mother about what it was like to adjust to living with someone else but, despite his lingering curiosity, had never plucked up the courage to broach the subject. When reading the obituaries of people, actors in particular, who'd been married multiple times, his imagination was always stirred. But, just like his mother, they were dead so he'd left it a bit late to quiz them and, had they been available, he was unsure exactly what it was he wanted to know.

Recently, on his morning walks he'd invented a harmless game where he imagined he was married to the first woman he passed in the street. Very occasionally, he'd pass someone he considered to be a possible candidate (late thirties, well turned out, sensible shoes, not too fat, not too thin, a bit shorter than him) but he only ever allowed himself a fleeting glance and, of course, never plucked up the courage to speak to them.

'Come on then, let's look at your list,' Julie said, finishing her porridge and getting up to rinse the bowl under the tap. 'I promise not to laugh.'

Duncan, looking sheepish, produced a single sheet of paper and slid it across the kitchen table. Julie picked up the page and, glancing anxiously at the clock on the wall, said, 'I must go or I'll be late.'

She read Duncan's list:

1. Become an exhibitionist - learn to tap dance.
2. Become a gambler - learn to play poker.
3. Become a blurter - start saying what I really think (and to hell with the consequences).
4. Become a risk-taker - rob a bank.

'Why on earth would you want to do any of these things? Anyway, you're a hopeless dancer, no sense of rhythm.'

'I just thought,' said Duncan sounding far from convinced,

'I'd got myself into a bit of a rut, that I should try to be more adventurous.'

Julie threw back her head and laughed. 'What *you,* adventurous? I'll believe that when I see it!'

'You promised not to laugh,' said Duncan miserably.

'I couldn't help myself. The idea of you doing any of these things is absurd. You're far too set in your ways. Anyway, I must rush.' Julie put on her coat and picked up her bag.

'I'm determined,' Duncan said wistfully, 'to try some new things before it's too late. You'll see.'

Julie smiled, gave him a peck on his furrowed brow and was gone.

Julie was, of course, right. Duncan's resolve failed him and he continued with his routines, taking comfort in their familiarity. Often, however, he emerged from his study at 4.30 expecting to welcome Julie back with the usual cup of tea only to find she hadn't yet returned from school. She always had plausible explanations: she'd been delayed by a staff meeting, a demanding parent had wanted to see her, she had volunteered to help convert a corner of the playground into a vegetable garden.

Then one day Julie said, 'I've seen no signs of you being more adventurous. Have you given up on the idea?'

'Not entirely. I'm still thinking about it.'

'Well, I can't bear the suspense. I'm leaving!'

'What do you mean? You're leaving? Where are you going?' Duncan was utterly flabbergasted.

'Simon has invited me to live with him in Tuscany.'

'Simon?'

'Yes, Simon, chairman of the governors. His father died recently and has left him a small fortune. He's buying a villa in Tuscany and I'm joining him.'

Suddenly, the harmless wife-spotting game Duncan played on his morning walks took on a new significance.

The Warning Sign

I've never known what to say when people ask me what I do for a living, at dinner parties for example. Often I buy time by inviting them to guess and they normally plump for a lawyer, accountant or doctor - not very imaginative. I suppose it's obvious that I'm some sort of professional person: well-heeled, well-spoken, wife and kids, nice car, a Knightsbridge address (I'm modest too!).

I usually laugh at their guesses and say 'I wish', flirting with the idea of stringing them along by telling them I own a quarry or a night club. Or, better still, that I earn my living by doing something really mysterious, perhaps as a soothsayer or a water diviner. But, alas, I know I wouldn't be able to sustain these untruths for long so I come clean and tell them the truth: I'm an ME, a Meetings Expert - a revelation that, quite under-standably, is invariably met with complete incomprehension.

Recently, for instance, at a private viewing in a Bloomsbury art gallery, I struck up a conversation with a woman who told me she was an actress who happened to be 'resting' at the moment. She was in her early sixties (though I would never have guessed) and explained how it was increasingly difficult for older woman to get television and film work. Naturally, I commiserated and then, after a short silence, the inevitable happened: she asked me what I did. The ensuing conversation went like this:

'I'm a meetings expert. I help people improve the effectiveness of their meetings.'

'A meetings expert? I've never heard of that. What sort of meetings?'

'Business meetings, management meetings, that sort of thing.'

'Goodness. And you can earn a living doing that?'

'Yes, I charge fees for my services.'

At this point most people shake their heads in disbelief and change the subject, asking, for example, if I ride or play golf or have dogs or have a place in the country. But this woman persevered.

'Really? That's incredible.'

'Yes, I sometimes have to pinch myself to believe it's true, but it's lucrative work and for the most part it's interesting and often entertaining.'

'Management meetings entertaining? Pull the other one. In the acting world meetings are invariably shambolic and time consuming.'

'Exactly, that's why I get hired. I never fail to recommend ways to reduce the number of meetings and, for those that survive my scrutiny, to halve the time they take and double what they accomplish.'

'I see, so really you're a sort of management consultant.'

'Yes, but since I specialise in meetings people don't think of me as a typical management consultant. It's fun and unexpected things often happen.'

'Fun? I'm still finding that hard to imagine. Meetings are so boring.'

'Not always. I'll give you a recent example. I was hired by the boss of a large organisation, it had better remain nameless, to help his directors improve the way they chaired meetings. As usual, I asked if I could observe some meetings to discover first-hand what sort of issues I might need to work on.'

'Oh, I see, you take a look first. But don't people find it odd having a stranger sitting in on their meetings?'

'Well, a one-way mirror would obviously be ideal but I make myself as unintrusive as possible. I just tuck myself in a corner and once the meeting gets underway people usually ignore me. Anyway, on this occasion one of the meetings I observed was chaired by a senior director. He briefed me beforehand and explained the meeting was a one-off to discuss how best to deal with an awkward situation they had with a trade union. He said it was all a bit fraught and asked for assurances that I'd keep everything I heard confidential.'

'Gosh, a bit hush hush. I like a bit of intrigue.'

'Yes, I was relieved to hear that the meeting wasn't going to be the usual routine thing with a set agenda. The director opened the meeting by explaining why I was there and urged the participants to take no notice of me. I sat in a corner by a large rubber plant. The leaves glistened under the lights and I couldn't help but wonder whose job it was to polish them.'

'A bit upmarket, eh?'

'Yes, the meeting was in the director's office, a large room with a round table. The discussion that ensued was rather circuitous with lots of conflicting ideas on how best to deal with the troublesome union reps. The director had some odd mannerisms that I duly noted in my log. For example, he often scowled and shook his head as if in disbelief and a couple of times he suddenly leapt up and strode around the table.'

'Goodness, sounds rather theatrical.'

'I told you meetings could be entertaining. The oddest thing was when he picked up a pencil - I'd noticed he had lots of them in a cut-glass tumbler on the table in front of him - and thrust it into the jaws of an electric pencil sharpener. He held it there while the sharpener made a whirring noise and the pencil was reduced to a stub. None of the participants seemed to think this in the least unusual.'

'That sounds really weird. And you get paid to watch this stuff?'

'Yep. I hope I'm not boring you?'

'Far from it. I *have* to know what happened next.'

'Well, soon after sharpening the pencil, the director completely lost it. He leapt up, ranting and raving, while everyone sat there with their heads down waiting for him to calm down. It was obvious that they were used to this bizarre behaviour and, sure enough, after a short while the director recovered his decorum and the meeting resumed as if nothing untoward had happened.'

'How extraordinary. I'm beginning to see what you mean about meetings being entertaining.'

'The same pattern - seize a pencil, grind it down in the pencil sharpener and, a short time after, go berserk - happened a number of times before the meeting adjourned for lunch. Two of the participants accompanied me to the company dining room and spent the whole time grumbling about the director. According to them he was impossible to work for, moody, short tempered and unpredictable. Normally, as an outsider with no axe to grind, I'm careful to keep quiet and remain impartial, but on this occasion I allowed myself to be drawn. I told them I'd detected a recurring pattern: pencil sharpening was always followed, after an interval of approximately three minutes, by the director blowing his top. They, of course, had become accustomed to both these things but were surprised to hear that the two behaviours might be linked.'

'Something I suppose it was relatively easy for you to spot as an uninvolved observer.'

'Precisely.'

'So, go on, what happened next?'

'After the lunch break the meeting resumed. The discussion was rather tortuous and it wasn't long before the director seized a pencil and ground it down in the sharpener. Unfortunately, the two managers I'd lunched with turned towards me and one winked and the other gave me a knowing smile. The director spotted this and demanded an explanation. Heads went down and no one said anything. After an awkward silence, I decided to come clean. I apologised and told the director that I thought sharpening a pencil was a sign of his mounting frustration with the lack of progress.'

'Goodness, that was brave. What happened next? He threw you out I suppose.'

'On the contrary, after a pause he asked me if I'd stay behind after the meeting. Naturally I assumed I had incurred his wrath, but after everyone had left he invited me to sit down and comment on the way he'd run the meeting. For the next hour I went through my notes giving him candid feedback. He lapped it all up, admitting that I was right about his regrettable displays of impatience. He thanked me profusely and promised to mend his ways.'

'That's a surprise. I thought you were going to say he punched you.'

'That's not all. A few weeks later I happened to pass the director in a corridor and, cheekily, I enquired if he'd stopped sharpening pencils.'

'Go on. What was his reply?'

'He said, 'Yes, thanks to your insightful advice, I'm a reformed character."

'So, he'd stopped behaving like an absolute bastard?'

'No, he'd stopped sharpening pencils.'

'But what about all the ranting and raving? That hadn't changed.'

'Well, you can't win them all. Come on, let's find another glass of champagne.'

On reflection, it might have been better to have told her I owned a quarry or a nightclub. Better still, that I was a sooth-sayer or a water diviner.

The Democrat

At long last they reached the final item on the agenda, AOB. As usual, the faculty meeting had been a rambling affair, inadequately chaired by Walter, the Professor of Psychology.

'Ladies and gentlemen, I'm pleased to announce that the university have entered into an arrangement with a distinguished group of professional artists.'

Walter paused, as if expecting this news to be greeted with rapturous applause. However, the members of the faculty sat impassively, seemingly unmoved, waiting for him to continue.

Walter was a caricature of a professor. He was a short, bald man, with thick horn-rimmed glasses and two front teeth that protruded over his bottom lip, making him look remarkably like a rabbit. He was fond of cardigans, complete with leather elbow patches, which he often buttoned up with the two sides out of alignment. He kept a pair of carpet slippers in his office and would put them on and shuffle around the department. Even when spruced up for special occasions, such as formal university dinners and degree ceremonies, he was incapable of looking tidy: his gown would hang lopsidedly off one shoulder, his suit, a row of biros protruding from the top pocket, was ill-fitting, his tie was invariably skewwhiff, his Hush Puppies were scuffed and his socks rarely matched.

Undaunted, Walter continued. 'Original works of art are to be loaned to the university on a cyclical basis and each faculty is invited to join the scheme. Every six months, if we wish, we can select a painting from those on offer.'

Nobody said anything and Walter added, somewhat lamely, 'Participation in the scheme is entirely voluntary.'

The Head of Experimental Psychology, a serious man more at home with rats in mazes than works of art, continued to doodle on his pad and, without looking up, asked, 'If we were to participate in the scheme, have you thought about where we would hang the painting? Presumably the artist in question will offer guidance on what constitutes a suitable site?'

'And,' the Head of Statistics chipped in, 'would we be liable for the safe keeping of the painting? Suppose a disgruntled student damaged it?'

'And,' the Head of Psychometric Testing asked, 'how will we agree which painting to select from those on offer? With something so subjective, reaching a consensus will surely be tortuous.'

'Yes,' the Head of Ethics added, 'we'll certainly need to agree on a process of elimination.'

Walter, disappointed that the scheme hadn't been enthusiastically embraced, and feeling wrongfooted by queries he hadn't anticipated, suggested it might be best to postpone further discussion until the next meeting.

He shuffled back to his office, gloomily reflecting on the cussedness of human beings. Theoretically he valued diversity but in practice he found accommodating disparate views and steering people towards a consensus nothing short of a nightmare. He always leant over backwards to avoid imposing his views or making decisions that could be construed as autocratic. His strong preference was to act as an impartial sounding board, encouraging people to explore the pros and cons of various options, gently allowing a consensus to emerge.

The members of the faculty had a soft spot for Walter but they enjoyed playing devil's advocate at the monthly meetings and watching him become increasingly discombobulated. Most of them were indifferent to the invitation to select paintings, but welcomed it as an opportunity to have fun and watch Walter gradually lose his grip on the proceedings.

In preparation for the next meeting, Walter, keen to find a way forward, sent each faculty member images of the first batch of six paintings on offer, inviting each of them to indicate their first, second and third choices. He urged them to do this independently without conferring. But when the results came in, Walter was dismayed to discover that no clear consensus had emerged: the choices were spread more or less evenly amongst the six paintings.

He wondered what to do for the best. Perhaps he should just go ahead and choose his favourite painting? But, as usual, he was wary of imposing his will. Or might it be best quietly to take some individuals aside and prevail upon them to change their choices? But that would amount to rigging the vote, leaving him open to accusations of corruption. Perhaps he should drop the whole idea? But how would he explain his change of heart to the Vice Chancellor, especially as he had been so effusive in welcoming the scheme?

He decided there was no alternative but to come clean, share the inconclusive data at the next meeting and invite suggestions on the best way forward.

Before the meeting, Walter felt strangely apprehensive. He was worried that his usual democratic approach would result in more unruly behaviour. It didn't help that the night before the meeting he had experienced an unsettling dream: Edvard Munch's painting of *The Scream* had been stolen whilst on loan to his department!

The next day, poor Walter arrived looking even more dishevelled than usual. Nervously, he broke the news about the impasse and invited suggestions on how best to proceed. After an inconclusive discussion about whether to have a second round of voting with some form of proportional representation, the Head of Statistics, with no particular axe to grind, suggested that the task of selecting a painting should be delegated to a sub-committee.

Relieved to have found a potentially promising way forward, Walter asked for volunteers to serve on the sub-committee. Hands shot up: everyone clamoured to join! Walter, surveying the sea of hands, looked utterly crestfallen, his chin wobbling slightly beneath his buck teeth.

There was an awkward silence.

Eventually the Head of Ethics, an empathetic woman with adopted children, came to the rescue. 'Professor, in the circumstances, I think we should invite you to choose a painting and we should all agree to abide by your decision.'

By now everyone had grown weary of the mischief-making and the proposition went through on the nod.

Walter slept well that night, secure in the knowledge that the decision to allow him to choose the painting had been reached democratically. His faith in human nature had been restored.

The Headmaster

I've just had my 93rd birthday. A surprise really - I never expected to live this long. Funny how young children and us oldies are so keen to divulge our ages. A few years back my late wife and I went on a Saga cruise and it was noticeable how many strangers in their nineties were falling over themselves (not literally), to say how old they were. And now I'm doing it: couldn't wait, even in the first sentence!

Unfortunately my dear wife died two years ago. Nothing dramatic, just the usual slow decline into frailty. We'd been married for nearly 66 years, so losing her was a bit of a wrench. An understatement really, but you know what I mean. I'm lucky to have a daughter and grandchildren living not far away who pop in from time to time to check up on me. I'm happy enough pottering around doing light housework and a bit of gardening.

We'd downsized and moved to a bungalow when my wife couldn't manage the stairs. Grab rails fitted everywhere. They're a bit unsightly and they remind me of my wife struggling. I was going to have them taken out, but my daughter says no, I might need them. I suppose she's right. I do use the handrail to help me up the two steps to the front door when I'm carrying shopping. The steps are a nuisance but we need them in case of flooding from the nearby river.

Downsizing was a wretched business, but it had to be done. The worst thing was sorting out my books. I had quite a collection, history books mostly. The local Oxfam shop took them. They even sent a van to pick them up. I only had to phone to say some books were ready and they came with empty cardboard boxes and took them away. In the end they must have had an impressive history section. I never went to look in case I couldn't help myself and started to buy back my own books.

Anyway, none of this is relevant to what I want to tell you.

Before I retired I was headmaster of a boy's prep school in East Sussex. We lurched from one crisis to another, financial problems mostly and some of a more smutty nature, but in our modest way we were successful. Our leavers often gained entry to decent schools, Marlborough, Stowe, Winchester, Wellington and so on. Even a couple of bright boys got into Eton and Charterhouse, but that was exceptional.

When I took over we had some teachers who were well past their sell-by-date, coasting complacently towards retirement. I got rid of the English teacher straightaway. The poor man was clearly an alcoholic and I dismissed him on the spot when he was caught in a drunken stupor one Wednesday afternoon when he was supposed to be teaching. The French teacher had to go too, an absurd little man too fond of hitting the children with a ruler. There were other casualties in my early days, and I got a reputation for being ruthless, but we gradually got there.

I persuaded the trustees to give me a free hand and I recruited a lot of young teachers who were keen to stay for a few years, make their mark and move on. Of course there were some exceptions amongst the old guard. A married couple who looked after the reception class had been at the school for over fifteen years and were brilliant. The parents loved them. The chaplain was an asset too. He doubled up as the music teacher and organised concerts and the school plays. We had some wonderful productions. I was always keen on promoting music. We had a policy that every child should learn to play an instrument.

The maths teacher, Martin Jackson, was another one who preceded my arrival. To be honest, at first I was doubtful about him because he was a bit of an odd ball. Early forties, a bachelor, not a conventional dresser, T-shirts and sandals most of the time- sandals with socks too, which I've always considered a no-no. And he had a beard - a big bushy one. I have to admit that I've always been a bit wary of people with beards. A silly hangup of mine. I always think they must be hiding something. But there was something a bit creepy about him. He had a way of standing too close, violating your body space. My wife used to feel edgy when he was around and get cross with me for allowing him to ingratiate himself.

But even though I initially had my doubts about Martin, and kept a close eye on him for some time, I was wrong about him. Not only was he very good at teaching mathematics, even to children with dyscalculia, he was also brilliant with the cubs and at games. Cricket, rugger, athletics, he'd spend hours of his free time patiently coaching the boys to good effect.

In his spare time he was a potter. He had his own kiln in a disused garage on the estate. I don't profess to know anything about pottery but he produced some that people seemed to rate. He used to sell them at school fetes, and a craft shop in the village stocked them on a sale-or-return basis. And they sold! He got quite a reputation locally. My wife bought a couple of his pots. They're still here; quite big, a pale grey glaze, with narrow necks. They're just decorative, never been used.

When my deputy head took early retirement - another triumph getting rid of him, but that's another story - despite my wife's reservations, I offered the post to Martin. But, to my surprise, he turned it down.

'Thanks, head, I really appreciate that, but I've been thinking for some time that I ought to move on. A bigger school perhaps, preferably in Cumbria where I could do some serious hiking and a bit of rock climbing.'

'Are you sure?' I asked, making no attempt to conceal my disappointment. 'If you stayed on here as deputy you'd almost certainly get the headship when I retire.'

'I'm guessing that'll be a good few years from now.' He smiled. He had a supercilious smile, as if he knew something you didn't know. It was disconcerting. 'No, even though I'll be sorry to go, I think it best to make the move while I'm still young enough to carve out a career elsewhere.'

'What about your kiln and your pot making gear?'

'I'll take them with me. Actually there is quite a thriving potting fraternity in Cumbria.'

And that was that. He would not be persuaded. I wished him luck with his job hunting and assured him of my support and promised him a glowing reference.

Afterwards I sat gazing out of my study window remembering how, when I'd first accepted the headship, I had fully intended to stay for a few years and move on. But I'd settled into the job and left it too late. Anyway, once I'd sorted out the dead wood and got things running smoothly, I have to admit it all got too comfortable. We had a house in the grounds, my wife and the kids loved it, especially in the vacations when, apart from the bursar and maintenance people, we had the place to ourselves. Though I say it myself, the reputation of the school slowly improved and, even though there were always problems to sort out, generally speaking things were on an even keel.

A couple of terms later Martin told me he'd been offered a post as head of maths at a large coeducational secondary school in Workington. I, of course, congratulated him without disguising my regret at losing him.

We gave him a good send off. The children clubbed together (well, their parents did!) and gave him a pair of climbing boots. Everyone signed a huge card painted by the art class. We even staged a concert where, between pieces of music, children read short pieces of appreciation and the chairman of the trustees made a speech. It was all very moving. I couldn't help thinking it was rather like a memorial service.

I recruited a new maths teacher very easily, a young fellow just out of teacher training with an Oxford degree. Then, after only one term, I had an unexpected phone call from Martin. After exchanging the usual pleasantries he said, 'I'm phoning to ask if you'll have me back.'

'How so?' I asked. 'Things not working out as you expected?'

'Yes, you could say that. It's not the same. I know it sounds soppy but I miss you all. It's like being permanently homesick. I keep telling myself it's silly, but I can't shake it off.'

I'd have loved to have been in a position to take him back, but I had to tell him that his old job had been filled and there were no staff vacancies. He didn't say much, just listened. I heard him sigh before he said, 'Thank you, head. It was worth a try. I hope you didn't mind my asking.'

I promised I'd let him know immediately if the situation changed and the call ended amicably.

I'm telling you all this now, over thirty years after the event, because at long last I'm sorting through some of my wife's things. I'll admit that I've been procrastinating over this. Some time ago my daughter kindly went through my wife's wardrobe and distributed clothes, shoes, handbags and so on to various charity shops. Actually, my daughter is being very helpful with decluttering. She persuades me I don't need to keep all sorts of things that were my wife's, including the two pots made all those years ago by Martin. She says they might fetch something on eBay.

Anyway, yesterday my daughter turned one of the pots upside down to see if Martin had signed and dated it, and an envelope fell out addressed to me. It had been opened and inside was a letter I'd never seen. This was a surprise because it was quite unlike my dear wife to keep things from me. Totally out of character in fact. Throughout our long marriage we'd always been open with each other and, so far as I was aware, had no secrets. Clearly, I was wrong in this instance.

The letter was written by Martin a few days after he'd phoned me.

Dear Headmaster,

I hope you will forgive me for pestering you (and thank you for being so gracious when I phoned) but I just want to emphasise how much I wish to return. I quite understand that my previous job is no longer available but I'm prepared to accept any position, however lowly, so long as you'll have me back. It's hard to explain how much I regret my decision to leave, but it is clear to me that it was a terrible mistake which, with your help, I wish to reverse.

PLEASE may I come back?

Yours sincerely
Martin Jackson

I sat pondering this cry for help wondering, if I'd seen it at the time, whether I'd have appreciated how desperate he was. Might I have taken him back even though we had our full quota of teachers? Would the arrival of such a pathetic letter, so soon after our phone conversation, have alerted me to the gravity of the situation? If I'd seen it, might I have predicted what might happen?

I read the short letter again. Why on earth would my wife have hidden it from me? It wasn't unusual for her to open the post, amongst her many duties she acted as my unpaid personal secretary, but to have concealed it and said nothing. Very strange. Of course, poor Martin must have wondered why I hadn't responded. Why I'd ignored his letter. Perhaps not getting a reply was a contributory factor. Or might my wife have replied on my behalf telling him there were no vacancies?

Anyway, as you must have guessed by now, things didn't end well. A few months after my telephone conversation with Martin, his sister rang to say had I heard the news? Martin had driven from Workington to her house in Devon and, without hinting what he was going to do, or leaving a note, he hanged himself in her garage.

If only I'd seen that letter, might things have worked out differently?

The Crafts Meeting

People arrived looking apprehensive, not quite sure what they'd let themselves in for. They were welcomed by a cheerful lady who showed them where to put their coats and introduced herself as Belinda, their self-appointed convenor.

'Thank you all for coming,' she beamed. 'I've been recuperating after a short stay in hospital, a minor procedure, I'll spare you the details. Thankfully my surgeon assured me I could count on a few more years and, while I lay there contemplating what to do with the rest of my life, I resolved to seize the initiative, to dither no longer; I'd start a crafts group.

She paused as if expecting a round of applause but her guests remained wary, feeling their way.

Undaunted, Belinda continued. 'Yes, my idea is to form a crafts group and thank you all for showing an interest.' Belinda beamed again, disguising her disappointment that no one was looking particularly eager. She continued. 'Though I say it myself, I've always been good with my hands.' She held her hands aloft and wiggled her fingers, leaving her guests to wonder what marvels they were capable of creating. 'Of course, crafts is a vague term covering a multitude of different activities, some intricate, some messy, some requiring equipment.'

Belinda paused again to allow imaginations to run riot. But still everyone sat there, slow to warm up, biding their time. 'So, we will need to agree what is feasible given that this, my dining room, is going to be the venue and this table,' she patted it fondly, 'our working surface.'

Eight people were gathered round the table - a bit of a squeeze. Another lady spoke.

'I'd better introduce myself. I'm Diana, people call me Di,' and I'm the person who coordinates all the groups and liaises with the convenors who, as you know, are all volunteers. I'm here to support Belinda and to offer whatever encouragement I can.'

'Thank you, Di,' Belinda beamed. 'Well, shall we go round the table and find out what crafts people have in mind? Who would like to kick off?' Belinda looked pointedly at the person sitting on her immediate left.

It worked.

'Thank you. My name is Alexandra. When I was a little girl I used to make collages out of pressed flowers. My idea is to do that again, though I know some people think it's wrong to pick wild flowers.' Alexandra looked apprehensive, as if bracing herself for disapproval.

'Why, I think that's a lovely idea,' said Belinda, writing 'pressed flowers' on the pad in front of her. 'Who's next?'

'My name is Janet and I want to make wire animals. I saw some in a craft shop recently. They were robins with little red cardboard hearts and I thought to myself, they'd be fun to make. I fancy making giraffes with their lovely long necks or elephants with their big ears and trunks.'

'Splendid, splendid! And kangaroos would be fun,' added Belinda. 'You could have a pocket with a baby kangaroo peeping out.' She beamed her approval, making another note on her writing pad.

'And penguins, they'd be easy to make,' added Alexandra, warming to the occasion.

'Yes, animals fashioned out of wire, that's a definite winner,' said Belinda, oozing enthusiasm. She looked at the next person, a small pinched lady.

'My name is Lynn. I'd like to make glove puppets with heads made out of papier mâché. I used to have some glove puppets when I was growing up, my granny made them, and now I've got some grandchildren of my own, I thought it would be fun to give them as presents.' Lynn looked round the room searching for support.

'Oh, that's interesting,' another woman piped up. 'I had a similar idea and thought it would be fun to make face masks out of old newspapers. You paste them together in layers. They could be decorated with feathers and bright colours.'

'I must confess I've always found masks a bit spooky,' said Belinda. 'I was once on holiday in Venice during the Carnival when everyone wore masks. It haunts me. Lots of grotesque black ones with huge beaks and cat masks worn by effeminate men. Really scary.'

'Well,' said the woman who had suggested mask making, 'I certainly don't want to make masks that are scary. I want to make decorative masks for kids to wear at parties.'

'Add it to the list, Belinda,' said Di, amiably. 'At this stage we are just gathering ideas, not evaluating them.'

'Yes, quite right,' said Belinda, suitably chastened. 'What other ideas do we have?' She looked at the women who had not yet contributed.

'My name is Debbie and I want to make brooches out of felt.'

Before anyone could react, a loud electronic chime interrupted the proceedings.

'That's the front door,' Belinda explained. 'Excuse me while I see who it is.'

She returned a few moments later with a man in tow. Everybody looked at him, astonished that a man should gate crash the group. He was an extraordinary sight, with a large bushy beard and a black patch over one eye.

'Sorry I'm late. Walked here and missed my turning.' He had a deep, unusually loud and booming voice.

'Better late in this world than early in the next,' giggled Belinda. 'We are just going round the table finding out what people would like to make,' Belinda explained. 'Would you like to catch your breath or are you ready to tell us what craft you'd like to undertake?'

'By all means. In for a penny, in for a pound! It's Harry by the way. Well, I'm into carpentry and I thought it would be fun for us to make articulated fish.' He whipped one out of his inside pocket and plonked it on the table. There it sat slightly quivering.

'Goodness!' exclaimed Belinda, 'it looks as if it's real. How on earth did you make it?'

'Trade secret, I'm afraid,' laughed Harry, tapping the side of his nose with his index finger, an action that revealed that his third and fourth fingers were missing.

'But you'd need to show us how to make them or your idea would be a non-starter,' Di interjected. 'The whole idea of forming a crafts group is to introduce each other to new crafts.'

'Well,' said Harry, 'I didn't for a moment think that you lovely ladies would want to get your dainty little hands dirty actually making them. You see, it's quite a palaver. I use a band saw and have an extractor to get rid of the sawdust. It's advisable to wear a mask and goggles too.'

'So,' said Belinda, 'why are you suggesting something so impractical?'

'And it's dangerous,' Harry continued, undaunted. 'As you can see I've had a number of unfortunate accidents. All my own fault. I damaged my eye - I always wear goggles now, a clear case of shutting the stable doors after the horse has bolted, eh? And the band saw sliced off two of my fingers before you could say Jack Robinson. I was momentarily distracted when our kitten jumped onto my back. Gave me one hell of a fright.'

People gazed at Harry as if he were an alien from outer space.

'I'm sorry,' said Di, 'but I have to agree with Belinda. Why are you suggesting an activity which, by your own admission, is inappropriate and potentially harmful?'

'Because I thought that if I did all the hard work and produced the fish, you ladies might like to colour and varnish them. They look lovely painted in bright colours and the varnish gives them a lovely sheen.'

After a stunned silence, when even Belinda was momentarily lost for words, a woman who had not spoken before, piped up. 'That's a bit rich! If I've understood you correctly, you are proposing to have all the fun making the fish using some secret technique, and expect us to sit here embellishing them for you. Well, I for one would rather busy myself with my chosen choice of craft: canvas work.'

'Yes,' added Lynn, 'I have no wish to be rude, but I think you should decorate your own fish. Don't expect us to do it for you.'

'Steady on. No need to get uppity,' retorted Harry, quick to take umbrage. 'I thought you ladies would enjoy decorating my fish.'

'Well, you thought wrong!' said Lynn. 'We are not prepared to be your lackeys. I'm sure others will agree with me.' She looked around the table for support.

'Yes,' agreed Alexandra, 'I'd rather busy myself doing my pressed flowers.'

'And,' added Janet, 'I still fancy making wire animals.'

Harry rose to his feet, picked up his fish and moved towards the door, where he paused, turned, and glared at the room full of women. 'I know when I'm not wanted. Thanks for nothing!' Then he was gone.

No one tried to stop him.

'Goodness,' said Belinda, 'apologies for that. Not at all what I was expecting when I suggested forming a crafts group.'

'Not your fault,' said Di. 'You couldn't have possibly anticipated such a bizarre intervention. Shall we resume going round the table?'

'Yes, of course,' said Belinda, recovering her decorum. 'Just to recap,' she consulted her list. 'So far I have: pressed flowers, wire animals, glove puppets, masks, felt brooches.'

'Not forgetting canvas work,' added the lady who had been the first to object to painting Harry's fish.

'Ah yes, of course, canvas work.' Belinda looked up and

laughed. 'You must admit it all sounds a bit tame doesn't it? Shall we get Harry back and tell him all is forgiven?'

Seven pairs of eyes stared blankly back at her. Nobody even smiled.

The Swoop

When it first started, Lucy decided it would be best to ignore it. She just carried on reading her book before turning off the light and curling up under the duvet with a pillow over her head. It was always the same: gentle tapping on the window accompanied by tuneless whistling, always after dark and only when her husband, Tom, was away.

But Lucy remained calm, confident she'd locked the front and back doors and closed all the downstairs windows. She hoped that the prankster, whoever he was (she assumed it must be a he), would soon give up.

'Bloody hell, it happened again?' Tom, home from a business trip, shook his head in disbelief. 'We could install a camera and catch the bugger red-handed.'

Lucy pursed her lips, a mannerism Tom loved. 'Thanks for the thought, but it's not worth the expense. He's harmless. If I don't react he'll soon get bored.'

'If you're sure. I hate to think of you alone in the house and not feeling secure.'

But, often after an absence of a few weeks, the tapping and whistling resumed.

Lucy, in her early thirties, still with the trim figure of a sixth former, was an optician at the local branch of Specsavers. Customers appreciated her professionalism as she subjected their eyes to various tests, her quiet voice guiding them through the process and explaining the results. After work, she sometimes joined a couple of the receptionists, Lyla and Mel, for a quick drink in the pub a few doors away from the opticians. They were younger than her, both sporting false nails and eyelashes, and Lucy was amused by their exploits on Bumble and short lived-romances. By comparison Lucy, married for three years to Tom, felt unadventurous and dowdy.

One day, unable to compete with Lyla and Mel's hilarious stories of disastrous blind dates, Lucy told them about her prowler.

'You mean that after you've gone to bed, he taps on the window?' Lyla's eyes opened wide as if she was bracing herself for a puff test.

'Yes, it's always the same, whistling and tapping on the sitting room window immediately beneath the bedroom.'

'Gosh! I wouldn't sleep a wink,' Mel exclaimed. 'What does Tom do? Go after him with a baseball bat?'

Lucy shook her head. 'It only happens when he is away. He says we should install security lights or a camera.'

'And you've no idea who it is?'

'Not a clue, except that it must be someone who knows when Tom is away.'

'Ah, a work colleague or a neighbour perhaps?'

'Maybe. Anyway, I'm sure it's best to ignore it and not give him the satisfaction of thinking I'm getting the jitters.'

'I'm amazed you can do that,' said Lyla. 'I'd definitely have the screaming heebie-jeebies if it happened to me.'

Despite Lucy's stoicism, the tapping and whistling continued, always when Tom was away on one of his business trips. It was puzzling. Why would anyone want to do it? What kicks could they possibly be getting out of it? She'd examined the small flower bed immediately outside the sitting room window looking for tell-tale signs: footprints perhaps or a dropped handkerchief. But there was no indication that anyone had loitered there. She'd even checked the windowpane to see if she could spot any fingerprints. Nothing.

One day, during their weekly phone call, Lucy told her mother about the prowler.

'My dear, why haven't you told me before? That's really scary. You must report it to the police.'

'I didn't want to worry you, and anyway it's harmless, just a nuisance. I don't think the police would be interested. They've better things to do.'

'Nonsense! You *must* report it. What does Tom say? Surely he's worried knowing he's leaving you alone in the house with someone spooky outside.'

'But nothing ever happens. I just ignore it and eventually he gives up and goes away.'

'Well, I definitely think you should report it.'

So, Lucy did.

Two police officers came. They sat in the kitchen and Lucy made them cups of tea: green tea for the female inspector and builder's tea, with a dash of milk and a spoonful of sugar, for her male companion.

'Sorry, but I have to ask, you're quite sure you aren't imagining it?

'No, there's definitely someone there tapping on the window and whistling.'

'Not a tree branch blowing in the wind?'

'No, there's nothing that could tap the front window except a person.'

'Have you any idea who'd want to do this? Have you fallen out with a neighbour or anything like that?'

'No, our immediate neighbours on both sides are elderly and other people in the road are just ordinary, friendly acquaintances. None of them seem in the least bit creepy'

'I'm afraid you can never tell,' the inspector said, pushing her spectacles up her nose. Lucy had already noticed they needed adjusting and wondered if she should offer. 'You say it only happens when your husband is away for the night. How would anyone know he was away?'

'I suppose they'd notice his car wasn't there.'

'But you say it doesn't *always* happen when your husband is away?'

'That's correct. Sometimes it doesn't happen for weeks and I start to think he must have given up and found something better to do.'

'Hmm. Does your husband always take the car when he goes away?'

'Usually yes, but not always. When he goes abroad he leaves it parked in its usual place and takes a taxi to the airport.'

'And can you recall any occasions when your husband's car has been parked outside and the prowler has come?'

'Sorry, but I'm really not sure. He just comes and goes. It's intermittent, there doesn't seem to be a definite pattern.'

'Well, the presence or absence of your husband's car seems to be a key factor. I suggest you try an experiment. Park the car somewhere else so that the prowler thinks your husband is away. My guess is that the prowler, if there is one, will assume the coast is clear. Try that and let me know the outcome.'

Tom was a bit reluctant, grumbling that parking the car in another street would be inconvenient, but Lucy persuaded him to try it. 'Don't you see, it means that if the prowler comes, you'll be here and you can go down and confront him.'

'Yeah, I guess so,' said Tom, sounding far from convinced.

Tom parked the car two streets away. A man protested that Tom was taking up his usual parking place but Tom said he was within his rights and showed him his residents' parking permit.

Then they waited to see what would happen. But it was a bit of an anti-climax: nothing happened, no prowler, no tapping, no whistling. Nothing untoward.

Lucy became pregnant (they had been trying for a baby for some time) and memories of the prowler slowly faded as Lucy succumbed to bouts of early morning sickness. Tom moved his car back to its usual parking place.

Some weeks passed. Then one night, when Tom's car was away having its annual service, and they were tucked up in bed, Lucy reading and Tom already asleep, the tapping began. It was gentle at first, so gentle that Lucy wasn't sure she'd heard it. Then it gathered momentum and became louder and Lucy was in no doubt. She nudged Tom. 'Listen, can you hear that? It's the prowler. He's back.'

Tom put on his dressing gown and, without switching on any lights, crept downstairs. He paused in the hallway, listening hard, but could hear no tapping. As stealthily as he could, he released the security chain on the front door, turned the yale lock, pulled the door open and stepped outside. There was nothing there, just the usual line of parked cars glistening under the streetlights.

Tom locked up again and went back upstairs. 'Are you quite sure you heard something? If so, by the time I'd got down there he'd scarpered.'

'It was definitely him tapping. No doubt about it. Perhaps he heard you coming?'

'Impossible, I didn't make a sound.'

'I'll report it in the morning. The police asked me to tell them if it happened again.'

'No, don't bother. I tell you what, tomorrow night you go to bed at the usual time and I'll hide outside by the backdoor and see if I can catch the bugger.'

So, the next night that's what happened. Lucy went to bed with her book and Tom settled himself down on a canvas chair behind the dustbins with a rug over his lap.

Just as Lucy turned off her bedside light and snuggled down to sleep, the tapping started. Lucy rang Tom's mobile. No answer. She left a message. No response. The tapping continued, now accompanied by tuneless whistling. Lucy started to feel panicky. Where was Tom? Why wasn't he answering? Why wasn't he doing anything? Perhaps the prowler had attacked him? Should she go downstairs and investigate?

She rang 999 and asked for the police. She tried to stay calm as she gave her name and address and told them her predicament. A reassuring voice told her that a patrol car was in the area and would be with her soon. She was not, repeat not, to go outside and must keep all the doors and windows locked.

Lucy sat on the edge of her bed and waited. The tapping had stopped by now and it was eerily silent. Might her unborn baby be distressed by her pounding heart? Where was Tom? Why didn't he answer?

She jumped when the doorbell rang. The police? She hadn't heard the patrol car arrive or any slamming doors. Just total silence. The bell rang again and a voice shouted through the letter box, 'Police here, don't be alarmed. Please open the front door. We have apprehended your prowler.'

Lucy went downstairs gingerly, wondering if it might be a trap. She stood behind the front door, hesitating to open it. 'How do I know you're the police?' she shouted. 'I didn't hear you arrive.'

'Don't worry, love. We did a swoop, killed the engine and turned off the lights. We've got your man. Look here's my badge.' The letterbox opened and the policeman shone a torch on his ID.

Lucy, leaving the chain on the door as a precaution, opened the door a few inches. She was confronted by two burly police-men and, wedged between them, Tom looking sheepish.

'Tell them it's me,' said Tom. 'They won't believe me.'

'Is this your husband, mam?'

Lucy took the chain off the door and opened it wide. 'Yes, that's Tom. What's happened?'

'We found him hiding behind the dustbins. He says he fell asleep.'

'Yes,' said Tom, 'sorry, I was sound asleep.'

'Well,' said the policeman who seemed to be in charge (Lucy couldn't help noticing he had a lazy eye). 'let's hope this is the end of the matter.' He gave Lucy a wink as if to say, 'we all know what's been going on here'.

A few weeks later Lucy, her pregnancy proceeding according to plan, saw a report in the local newspaper about a man who'd been charged with stalking lone women and following them home. A couple of the victims were quoted in the article, one of them recounting how, after she'd gone to bed, he used to tap on her window.

Lucy showed the paper to Tom as soon as he returned from a business trip to Hartlepool.

'Bloody hell, I know that guy!' he exclaimed. 'He's the bloke who complained when I parked my car outside his house.'

The Padded Bench

There were a couple of reasons why I chose to have a go at sketching that particular painting. The first was laudable: I knew it would be one hell of a challenge. The second (to me of equal importance) was the proximity of a comfortable-looking padded leather bench.

Most of the seats in the National Gallery are unforgiving wooden benches, dark brown with no back rests, presumably designed to deter people from loitering or falling asleep. I know from bitter experience how easily physical discomfort, e.g. a numb bum, torpedoes higher functioning. It's Maslow's hierarchy all over again: basic stuff has to be tickety-boo before self-actualisation pulls into view. Hence my decision, taken a few years ago on my sixtieth birthday, to quit working outside, en plein air: too uncomfortable, crouching on my canvas stool, balancing everything on my lap, with the wind blowing and ants crawling up my legs.

Yep, the proximity of the leather bench was a major consideration - oh, let's be honest, *the* major consideration - when I chose to plonk myself in front of that painting. Plenty of other paintings nearby, Turners and Constables, would have been easier, but the leather bench was nicely placed immediately in front of this one. It was a large painting too, offering good visibility even when people loitered in front of it.

But I was under no illusions, it was a tough call: ten figures clustered round a glass thingy, with lots of contrasting light and shade, and masses of intricate detail. It looked more like a photograph than an oil painting, God knows how the artist pulled it off. I'd seen a reproduction of the painting somewhere before and vaguely remembered that it was something to do with the Industrial Revolution.

I read the notice beside the painting:

Joseph Wright of Derby 1734 - 1797, An Experiment on a Bird in the Air Pump, 1768

A lecturer demonstrates the creation of a vacuum to a family. A white cockatoo (an exotic bird, unlikely in fact to have been used for this experiment) is imprisoned in a glass flask from which air is being extracted by a pump. The candlelit setting is characteristic of Wright's interest in dramatic contrasts of light and shade.

Can't say that birds are my thing, but in my opinion, whoever dreamed up this experiment should have been reported to the RSPB (sadly, not possible. I've since looked it up: the Society didn't come into existence until 1889).

I sat down on the bench, just right, not too soft, and fished my large sketch pad out of my satchel. Security had taken a good look inside it at the entrance, but since it only contained a large pad of cartridge paper, I was let through with a nod. The pad balanced quite nicely on my knees. I always sketch using a propelling pencil with a soft lead (3B if you're curious, but I don't want to give away too many trade secrets). A propelling pencil saves you having to muck about with a sharpener.

Refusing to feel daunted by the accomplished Joseph Wright of Derby, I made a start, outlining the figures using very faint lines. I don't hold with rubbers. Knowing you can rub something out is a licence to be slapdash. Just think, if mistakes could be erased, murder, rape and pillage would be widespread and prisons wouldn't have been invented! So, no rubbers. No rulers either (oh lord, more trade secrets!).

It wasn't long before someone joined me on the leather bench - not a problem, plenty of space. At a stretch it could probably accommodate seven or even eight people, fewer if they were obese of course. Anyway, I just kept sketching and didn't look up. It's not that I'm anti-social, but I've found that if you ignore people and keep working they are more likely to have a quick gawp and move on. I've made the mistake before of getting sucked into lengthy conversations about this and that. It often starts with the passer-by asking a dumb question such as 'are you an artist?' I'm tempted to say, no, I'm a plumber, but that would probably spawn questions about why I was moonlighting when plumbers were in short supply. No, I've found it's better to come clean and curtail the conversation as quickly as possible.

Anyway, this time my companion just sat there, gazing at Wright's painting (I could see him out of the corner of my eye) and I was beginning to admire him for not disturbing me, when he sighed and, with a sideways glance, said, 'I see you're left-handed.'

I continued to sketch and replied, 'Ambidextrous actually, but I've always drawn using my left hand.'

As soon as I said this I knew I'd made a mistake. But I carried on sketching, resisting the temptation to turn and make eye contact. If I'd really wanted to chat I could have told him about my teacher at art school who used to bandage my left hand to stop me using it. But I just pressed on with the sketch, hoping the bloke would soon shove off.

'Ambidextrous, eh? That's unusual. I once read that only one percent of people are ambidextrous.'

I answered, 'Good to know I'm a rare species.' By now I realised I'd blown it, so I stopped sketching and looked at the guy sitting on my right. He was an elderly man, well, about my age probably, hard to tell because he was completely bald and had a white, bushy beard. He was dressed in black and was wearing what looked like a university gown. Beside him was a staff, made of dark wood and covered in carvings. 'Yes,' he added, 'but at least you're not that much of an oddball. Apparently ambidextrous people are far more likely to be male than female.'

Wary of being dragged into a debate about gender, I laughed and said, 'Fancy you knowing that!'

'Not at all, I'm full of useless pieces of information.'

We sat in silence for a while, he back to contemplating the painting and me busy sketching. Eventually he said, 'Care to hazard a guess about the connection between this painting and today's date, 28th April?'

'No idea. What's this, *Only Connect*? I hate quizzes.'

He chuckled. 'Apologies, an unfair question. I'll put you out of your misery. Today is Terry Pratchett's birthday and the cover design for his first Discworld book was a parody of this painting.'

I'm not a great reader. When people mention books I usually nod knowingly, pretending I've read them, or at least have heard of the authors. As it happens I *had* heard of Terry Pratchett because I knew he'd died of complications from Alzheimer's, same as my mum, but I don't go for fantasy stuff and hadn't read any of his books. I decided honesty was the best policy and said, 'No way I could have known that. I'm afraid I've never read any of Pratchett's books.'

My companion smiled. 'You don't know what you're missing,' and looked back at the painting, with a reverential sigh. It was a bit spooky really, him just sitting there, leaning on his staff, gazing at the painting. I sketched on but after a while the silence seemed awkward and, breaking my self-imposed rule, I said, 'I take it you're a fan of Pratchett's writing?'

'Yes, that's why I'm dressed like this. I'd be wearing my black fedora but they made me surrender it at the cloakroom. Said it would obscure people's view. Last year I came in my wizard outfit but they made me hand that hat in too.'

'Oh, so you come here often?'

'No, not often. Just on 28th April for the past few years.'

I nodded as if accepting that it was perfectly normal to sit, dressed in black, gazing at Wright's painting every 28th April. I carried on sketching anticipating further clarification but he fell silent and when I next looked round, he'd vanished.

On the padded bench, in the space he'd occupied, lay a small package addressed to me. I opened it, puzzled because I was sure I hadn't told him my name. Inside was a paperback, *The Science of Discworld* by Terry Pratchett. On the title page he'd written:

I'm shocked you've never read any of my books. Try this one - the first of 41.

Terry Pratchett

PS Good sketch. Never met a left-handed artist before.

Acknowledgements

Thanks to the members of my u3a writing group for all their help: Linda Ciardiello, Joy Smith and Astrid Thompson. Thanks to Robin Stuart-Kotze for volunteering to proofread and for his generous foreword. Thanks to Carol, my wife, for, well, everything!

About the Author

Dr Peter Honey worked as an occupational psychologist, specialising in interpersonal skills and lifelong learning. He is the author of many management books and self-assessment questionnaires, including the widely used Honey & Mumford *Learning Styles Questionnaire*. He is married and lives in Windsor.

Website: www.peterhoney.org